W9-BQS-995

DAUGHTERS OF THE MOON

the prophecy

Also in the

DAUGHTERS OF THE MOON

series:

1. goddess of the night
2. into the cold fire
3. night shade
4. the secret scroll
5. the sacrifice
6. the lost one
7. moon demon
8. possession
9. the prophecy
10. the talisman

DAUGHTERS OF THE MOON

LYNNE EWING

HYPERION/NEW YORK

 For information address Volo Books, 114 Fifth Avenue, New York, New York 10011-5690.

First Edition
3 5 7 9 10 8 6 4 2
Printed in the United States of America

Library of Congress Cataloging-in-Publication Data on file.

ISBN 0-7868-1891-3

Visit www.volobooks.com

For RZ1, Sylvia Weiss

PROLOGUE

1249 A.D.

The Keeper pulled the illuminated manuscript from its hiding place and spread it on the stone hearth. The golden border caught the fire's light, and its reflection looked like an eye flashing open. At once the illusion vanished, but something else caught the Keeper's attention, and the shock of it took his breath away. Within the enlarged first letter, the miniature of the goddess unlocking the jaws of hell had changed; her beauty was gone, replaced by the cruel gaze of a Follower. Was this another change the Scroll had wrought upon itself, or had someone tampered with its magic again?

The Keeper dipped his paintbrush in brown

pigment and began drawing a tree on the parchment, curving its limbs over and around the calligraphy until the words were hidden in a maze of twisting branches. For centuries he had devoted himself to uncovering this forbidden knowledge, and now he had assumed the duty of protecting it. He wished he could follow the Path, but the Prophecy was clear; only the child of a fallen goddess and an evil spirit could follow the steps without fear of the Scroll's curse.

Many had died trying to use its magic, but that wasn't the reason the Keeper now kept it hidden, denying its existence. A dangerous transformation had taken place. The Scroll had somehow come to life, as if the words written on the parchment had infused it with an instinct for survival. He could feel it now, alert and suspicious beneath his fingers.

When it was no longer watching him, he dropped his brush, grabbed a reed pen, dipped it into the glutinous black ink, and wrote one final instruction on the last page. His deception awakened whatever lived within the manuscript. Intense light shot through him with deadly force, binding his existence to that of the Secret Scroll for all time.

CHAPTER ONE

CATTY RAN DOWN THE sidewalk near the La Brea Tar Pits. The air was thick with the odors of asphalt and methane gas. She glanced over her shoulder to make sure no one was following her, then put on sunglasses and a cap before hurrying past two guys listening to thundering riffs of hard rock from a boom box.

She took a deep breath, trying to calm her nerves, then pulled *The L.A. Times* from her backpack and stared down at the photo of an illuminated manuscript. The Los Angeles County Art Museum had purchased the antique document from a man who had bought it at a swap meet.

Just last week the man had died. Now, the museum curator and a security guard were in the hospital on life support with the same flulike ailment. The parchment had been examined for radiation and toxins. The newspaper compared what was happening to King Tut's curse, but Catty blamed only herself. If she hadn't spent spring break in San Diego hanging out on the beach with her friends, she might have been able to prevent the man's death.

Catty had to do something, before another person died. The curse was real, but who was going to believe her if she told them? Then again, it wasn't as if she couldn't prove what she said, because she had a gift. But revealing her power of time travel could be risky. That left her no option. She had to steal back the Scroll.

She entered the museum through the monumental portal on Wilshire Boulevard and charged up the stairway, the skylight high above her. She turned toward the central courtyard and stopped. The plaza was filled with reporters and cameras. She hadn't expected so many potential witnesses.

A newscaster from channel seven was staring into the lens of a camera, giving a report. Catty hurried behind her, surprised to hear the reporter utter the word "Atrox." What did the museum people know?

Head down, she threaded her way through the crowd, then squeezed awkwardly past a man taking down audio equipment. She didn't need someone identifying her later. Still, she fantasized what it would be like to walk up to the podium, grab the microphone, and tell everyone the truth. She imagined their expressions when she explained that the manuscript revealed an ancient path for defeating a primal source of evil called the Atrox.

She smiled wryly, remembering the prophecy. *Only the child of a fallen goddess and an evil spirit shall inherit the Scroll.* She was that child, the Scroll's heir. Would they think she was evil, too, or would they want to help her? The answer didn't matter. She could never reveal her true identity without putting herself and her friends in danger.

Suddenly, her chest tightened with new

anxiety. The world might find out, anyway. According to the newspaper, Miori Amasaki had begun translating the Scroll. Already, sections of it had been printed in the *Times*. If Catty didn't steal it before the translation was completed, everyone would find out her secret. The thought terrified her. If government officials knew about the Daughters and their powers, they would assign a scientist to examine them. She imagined herself and her friends locked up on some remote military base, undergoing tests. She tried to brush the thought away as she stepped up to a security guard.

"I'm doing an internship with Ms. Amasaki," she lied. "Could you tell me where to find her office?"

"Lower level of the Hammer Building." The guard barely glanced at her.

Minutes later, the elevator doors rumbled open, and Catty stepped out, her pulse thudding in her temples. At the far end of the hallway the air rippled; it was as if her eyes were going in and out of focus. She took off her sunglasses and slipped them into her backpack. The illusion vanished.

She thought about the moon amulet hanging around her neck. It had been given to her at birth. Her best friends, Serena, Tianna, and Vanessa, each had one, too. She wished they were with her now, but she hadn't told them what she was doing. They would have insisted on coming with her, and she had been afraid the Scroll's curse might harm them. She couldn't put their lives in jeopardy—at least, not until she had a better plan than this one.

Satisfied that the charm wasn't alerting her to danger, she stepped off the elevator. If something had lurked at the end of the hallway, it was gone now. Maybe the undulating air had been the effect of her vision adjusting to the dimmer light inside. Still, she stepped slowly forward, listening for the furtive sounds of someone following her. She wasn't the only one searching for the Scroll, and the others were deadly and determined in their quest.

At last she found the right office. A nameplate read MIORI AMASAKI. She stared at the door, her heart pounding wildly. A gash near the lock made it look as if someone had forced something between the door and jamb to open it. She hoped she wasn't too late.

She started to turn the knob, when footsteps echoed down a distant corridor. Frantic, she looked for a place to hide, then tiptoed across the hall and slid into a restroom, careful not to let the door slam. She braced herself against the cold, tiled wall, closed her eyes, and took several deep breaths to quell her panic. She had never been that nervous defending herself against Followers, but stealing a million-dollar artifact was making her dizzy.

"Tu es dea, filia lunae," she whispered, trying to give herself courage. "You're a goddess, a Daughter of the Moon."

When she opened her eyes, she caught her reflection. A bruise streaked her jaw, and a long scrape slid down her right arm. She had made too many trips into the past, hoping to find the Scroll before the man purchased it. Her knees and back still ached from the many landings in a short period of time.

The footsteps tapped past the bathroom, hesitated, then hurried away.

Catty let out a sigh of relief, opened the door, and peered out. Whoever had been there was gone now. She slipped across the hallway and tested the doorknob again, expecting to find it locked. Instead, it turned in her hand. She eased inside, trying to push away her worries, and closed the door behind her.

The room was empty and quiet. Gray light came through a window that looked out on an ivy-covered embankment. Catty walked to a desk, the carpet absorbing her footfalls, and began rummaging through a stack of papers. *Atrox* was written across one sheet, as if the translator had been puzzling over the word's meaning.

The desk was locked. Quickly she found a paper clip, straightened it, and slid it into the keyhole. The metallic scratching sound made her fearful again that someone would discover her. At last she heard a click, and the first drawer opened.

A glint of gold caught her eye. The Scroll lay before her. She admired the detailed artwork on the borders, in which exotic beasts and birds with long feathers hid in twisting tree branches.

She picked up the manuscript. The parchment pulsed beneath her touch as if she had awakened it. She dropped it and stepped back, rubbing her fingers on her jeans to rid herself of the unpleasant sensation that the parchment had recognized her. She didn't recall having had such a feeling before. Perhaps Gerard de Molaire, the sorcerer who had hidden a spell within the Scroll, had channeled some kind of sinister energy into it. But then another thought came to her. Chris had given her the manuscript before, and maybe he had controlled it then.

Her heart sank. What had happened to Chris? The last time she had seen him, he had been pretending to be a student at La Brea High School. She shook her head. She couldn't believe the way she was still crushing on a guy she'd probably never see again.

She touched the parchment with the tip of her finger. The odd sensation was gone now. Maybe she had only imagined the strange stirring.

She opened her backpack and slipped the Scroll inside, but, as she started to leave, she became aware of someone standing in the far corner of the room, watching her.

CHAPTER TWO

"KYLE?" CATTY HATED the sudden squeal in her voice. This was all she needed. Now she had a witness.

"Hi, Catty." Kyle leaned against a bookcase, holding some computer printouts in his hands. He was grinning, and the cuffs of his jean jacket were black with dirt. Kyle had gone to La Brea High until he had been expelled. Now he went to Turney, but she still saw him at Planet Bang, hanging out with all his badass friends.

"What are you doing here?" she asked, ignoring his smirk. Why wouldn't he stop smiling?

"You're asking me?" he said, arching an eyebrow.

She hated his cocky attitude. His gorgeous looks made him a heartthrob, though. Girls were crazy about him, but he was a magnet for trouble. Rumors about him had been going around school even before he had been forced to leave. Then she remembered the deep gashes on the door. Had he broken in? What was his interest in the Scroll?

"You're prowling around where you don't belong, and you want me to explain what I'm doing?" He brushed his shaggy hair from his eyes. Bruises covered his knuckles as if he had been in a fight.

"You should have told me you were watching," she said, not backing down.

"Because . . . ?" He tilted his head, waiting for her to explain. When she didn't, he continued. "Because it's rude to watch someone steal a valuable piece of art? I apologize. I didn't know."

She rolled her eyes. "You don't understand—"

"Unlike you, I'm not looking for an

explanation." He frowned. "Just put the manuscript back."

She challenged him with her stare. There was no way she was going to let go of the Scroll now. She started to build her energy, in order to open the tunnel and escape through time, but then a thought came to her with a jolt. "You were going to steal the manuscript, weren't you?" Her eyes narrowed, watching him carefully.

"Sure," he answered sarcastically. "And that's why *you* have it in *your* backpack."

Anger flooded through her, and at the same time she was annoyed with herself for letting him distract her. If someone had come into the room right now, she would have been the one caught with the Scroll. "I know you broke in."

"And you didn't?" He looked down at the papers he was holding, as if dismissing her.

She stepped closer and yanked the pages out of his hand. "Why are you reading translations of the manuscript?"

He yanked the papers back, rolled them up tightly, then stuck them in his pocket. "Who am

I to turn down a pile of cash from a reporter who wants a scoop?"

"That's why you're here?" Catty asked. His answer seemed plausible, but she didn't believe him. "Someone bribed you to break the law?"

"I would love to stay and chat, but I, uh, don't really care." He started to walk away, but then his glance caught something below her neck, and he turned back.

She folded her arms over her breasts, a blush surging to her cheeks. In the dim light, she couldn't tell exactly what his eyes were focused on, but his stare was creeping her out. "What are you looking at?"

"Your necklace is shining." He gave her a curious look, then grabbed her moon charm before she could move out of the way.

"Ouch!" He let it go as if the metal had stung him. "What is it?"

Catty glanced down. Her amulet glowed in warning. Were Followers near? Or was there another reason she should be alert? She looked hard at Kyle. If he was a Follower, then he was only an Initiate—one of the kids who had turned to the Atrox hoping to be accepted into its congregation—because she couldn't feel him trying to control her with his mind. Was it possible that Kyle had planned to steal the Scroll as a way to prove himself worthy of becoming a Follower? He had that kind of bad-boy reputation, but she had never sensed anything evil about him. There was only one way to know for sure. She clasped his fingers to see if her moon amulet had burned his skin.

"Can I ask what you're doing?" he said, trying to pull free.

She held on to him tightly, breathing in the faint smell of turpentine and linseed oil from his clothes. His skin wasn't burned. She twisted his hand to force his palm down and was surprised by what she saw. Bruises didn't really cover his knuckles, and the cuffs of his jacket weren't black from dirt.

"You paint?" she asked, certain that he did. She'd never seen him in one of her art classes, but she recognized the stains of oil paints.

He snatched his hand away.

Before she could say more, she heard approaching footsteps on the other side of the door.

His eyes widened. "We have to hide." He eased back toward the corner near the floor-to-ceiling bookshelves.

Catty ignored his outstretched hand. She had what she had come for, and now she was going to travel into the past. Kyle would probably have a flash of déjà vu the next time he saw her, but he wouldn't remember what had just happened. When she went back in time, it was like rewinding a videotape and then recording over it.

He motioned for her to join him in the shadows.

She took off her cap, crammed it into her backpack, and then concentrated, feeling her eyes expand. Goose bumps rippled over her skin as power surged through her. The air pressure changed, and her hair bristled with static electricity, meandering snakelike around her head. Then the minute hand on her watch began spinning backward.

Suddenly, Kyle lunged forward and grabbed her wrist. "Are you trying to get us caught? If you stay in the middle of the room, they'll see you."

She squinted, restraining her power. If she left now, Kyle would go with her, and he would definitely have a memory of that. Without an outlet, her energy prickled painfully along her arms and legs. She sucked in air, then realized that Kyle was unzipping her backpack.

"Don't!" she whispered, too late.

He pulled out the Scroll and placed it back inside the desk as the doorknob turned.

She pitched forward, reaching for the Scroll. "You don't understand. I'm not really stealing it."

He caught her hand, closed the drawer, and yanked her back.

The door started to open, and the light from the hallway slanted across the carpet.

CHAPTER THREE

"THERE'S NO PLACE TO hide," Catty whispered, feeling panic rise inside her.

Kyle guided her toward the back of the room, his lips moving against her ear. "There's always a place if you're desperate enough."

Then, holding her tight, he squeezed between two bookcases, pulling her into a small niche. She tensed her body, trying not to press against him, but the recess was narrow and they were jammed together, his breath tickling her temple.

The overhead lights buzzed on and someone coughed.

Catty peered around Kyle's arm, straining her neck to see beyond the edge of the bookcase.

A woman stood at the desk, sniffling loudly. Catty wondered if the woman had seen the slash marks on the door. If so, she didn't act concerned. Instead, she pulled out a tissue, blew her nose, and then sat down, opening a laptop. Her fingers clicked across the keys. How long was she going to stay?

Kyle carefully pulled Catty back, his eyes intense with warning. She nodded, suddenly aware of his hands on her back. Her breath stopped. She had never stood this close to a guy before, not even Chris. She wanted to hate Kyle's embrace, but something stirred inside her, filling her with a sudden urge to kiss him. Kyle? Gross.

Other girls might be in love with him because of his looks, but Kyle wasn't Catty's type. She tried to pull her thoughts back to the Scroll.

Then a mischievous thought crossed her mind. Why not indulge a bit? As soon as this was over, she was going to go back in time and erase his memory anyway. Was that wrong? She'd be using him, but at the moment, she didn't care. She closed her eyes and pressed closer to him, enjoying his warmth. Did Kyle know what she was doing?

Her physical attraction to him baffled her. She didn't really know Kyle. Maybe loneliness caused this feeling. All her friends had guys. Vanessa had been going with Michael for a long time now. Jimena went out with Serena's brother, Collin, and Tianna had a steady boyfriend, Derek.

Catty was jealous even of the romance between Serena and Stanton, although their relationship was doomed. Stanton was a Follower and had sworn to destroy the Daughters. Only his love for Serena had stopped him so far.

She sighed. It was hard being the only one in their group who didn't have someone.

A clattering made her start, and even though Kyle tried to hold her back, she peeked out again.

The woman gathered the translations, slipped the Scroll into a case, and departed, locking the door behind her. Catty breathed a sigh of relief that the woman hadn't noticed the jimmied lock on the desk drawer.

Kyle spoke first. "She's gone. You can stop feeling my butt."

"I wasn't!" But her hands had slipped down to his jean pockets.

"You were," he teased.

She yanked away from him, stumbling back. "I didn't have any place to put my hands."

An easy smile crossed his face as he watched her.

"All right," she admitted. "But it's not what you think."

"What do I think?" He stepped closer.

She backed away. "I don't have a crush on you, like all the other girls."

"You don't?"

His stare flustered her. Did he expect her to come back and start making out with him?

"Bye, Kyle."

She wasn't going to stay, and she didn't care if he saw her leave. It wasn't as if he would remember it, anyway. She concentrated. Energy exploded inside her, and then a white flash filled the room, and a hollow darkness opened behind her.

"What the—!" Kyle rushed toward her.

"Adios," she shouted, enjoying the fear and surprise on his face.

She soared into the tunnel. She liked tumbling through the fizzing air, and even the sickly cabbage smell didn't bother her. She felt safe there. She glanced down at her glow-in-the-dark wristwatch. The hands weren't moving. She had probably broken it going back and forth in time so many times that day. She concentrated on stopping, and a slit of light opened in front of her. Immediately, she started plummeting down, bracing for another fall.

Sunlight flashed in front of her eyes, and the smell of coffee filled her nostrils. Where was she? She had planned on landing in the hallway, but she was outside somewhere. She dropped from the tunnel down to a place in the central courtyard at the museum, only two yards from an espresso kiosk. She waved her arms for balance, trying to land softly, and prayed no one saw her appear.

Her shoes hit the ground with a sharp jolt, pain raced up her spine, and her momentum made her unable to stop. She was going to smash into a steaming coffeemaker straight ahead.

Suddenly, someone stepped in front of her, and she slammed hard into his back, spilling his coffee.

"Sorry," she whispered and looked up.

Kyle stared down at her with his incredible blue eyes.

Catty looked around. She must have arrived back at the beginning of the press conference that had been breaking up when she had arrived at the museum earlier. She tried to calm herself. At least, no one seemed aware of the reason she had fallen against Kyle.

"You could have come up with a better way of getting my attention," Kyle said, interrupting her thoughts.

"Are you kidding me?" Anger bubbled up

inside Catty. "You have got to be the most obnoxious—"

He shot her an insolent look, then pointed down to the stains on his jeans. He grabbed a wad of napkins and began to blot the coffee spills.

"Whatever." She refused to apologize.

He tossed the wet napkins into the trash and walked away from her.

Catty took in a deep breath. She couldn't concern herself with Kyle. She had more important things on her mind. She shoved through the crowd, inching closer to the podium, but something made her glance back. Kyle was staring at her, as if he had known she couldn't resist one last look. Did he really think he was that great?

Then another thought shot through her, replacing her anger with apprehension. What was Kyle doing in the central courtyard? He should still have been downstairs in the basement office, or at least on his way there, shouldn't he? Regulators sent by the Atrox were also after the Scroll, and they could change their looks at will. Could Kyle be one?

CHAPTER FOUR

CATTY TENSED, HER eyes vigilant, searching the crowd for danger. She remembered her last encounter with the Regulators. They hadn't known then that she was the heir. This time, they would. But she could now recognize the strange static electricity their presence created. That made her wonder if they had become more cautious. Perhaps they had bribed someone like Kyle to follow her and stop her from taking possession of the Scroll.

The shrieking whistle of feedback interrupted her thoughts. She turned toward the podium. News reporters, photographers, New Agers, politicians, and religious leaders crushed closer, impatient to hear the statement that was about to be delivered.

A thin man leaned over the cluster of microphones. "Good morning," he said. He cleared his throat and continued. "We have good news. The health department and the biohazard team have examined the manuscript thoroughly and have come up with nothing to concern us. We simply have had the misfortune of having a flu epidemic hit us at the same time that the museum purchased this magnificent masterpiece. Although talk of a curse is certain to sell newspapers, let me assure you that the manuscript is nothing more than a piece of parchment with exquisite artwork." He held up his hands to fend off questions. "The arts council has decided to put the Scroll on display immediately, to dispel rumors of any curse. Thank you."

He breezed away and disappeared into the Anderson Building.

Catty's heart sank. What could she do now?

Once the Scroll went on display, it would be surrounded by security guards, motion detectors, closed-circuit TV, automatic locks, and an array of silent alarms. How was she going to steal it now? She rubbed her temples, trying to hold back tears.

"What's wrong?" Kyle was suddenly beside her, his hand resting on her shoulder.

"Nothing." She turned away from him, trying to think. Maybe if she went further into the past, she could steal the Scroll, but she felt that her power was too drained for such a long trip; her back still throbbed from the last landing.

"Catty?" Kyle moved in front of her. "Do you need a doctor? You slammed into me pretty hard."

She looked up, expecting to see mockery on his face; instead, he looked at her with real concern.

"I'm fine." She hurried away from him, anxiety ripping through her. She needed to find a place away from the crowd, so that she could travel forward a few minutes and get the Scroll before Ms. Amasaki took it from the room. She didn't need any curious reporter jumping into the tunnel with her.

What would happen if she couldn't steal the Scroll back and every word within it were translated? Would people go on a witch hunt for the Daughters?

CHAPTER FIVE

CATTY SLIPPED INTO the gift shop, away from the crowd, and focused her thoughts, struggling to open the tunnel. A tickle curled through her fingers, then died. She strained again, her temples throbbing as a headache set in, and tried to use her power.

Glass paperweights shimmied across the display case as the air around her grew heavier.

Shoppers turned, their eyes wide with fear.

"Earthquake," a woman whispered, pressing a hand over her heart, her face anxious.

Catty grabbed the edge of the counter, suddenly dizzy, her arms prickling as the energy disintegrated inside her. She had definitely pushed her power too far this time.

"You must have been in Northridge for the big one," the salesman said. He patted her hand, his manicured fingers cold. "Me, too. Now every little rumble scares the life out of me."

Catty flashed the man a weak smile, then adjusted her backpack and walked outside toward the Bing Building, her legs trembling and weak.

Only two hours had passed since she had returned from San Diego, but during that time she had traveled into the past and stayed there for at least eighteen hours, searching for the Scroll. No wonder she felt too jittery to think. She needed to eat and rest before she tried to use her powers again.

She stepped into the Plaza Café, where the smells of pizza and hamburgers hit her. Only then did she realize how hungry she had become. She waited in line. When it was her turn, she ordered fire-roasted veggies with extra olive oil.

She stuffed a blackened pepper into her mouth, poured a Coke, and went to find a place to sit.

Reporters crowded the small tables, their laptops open, fingers clattering across keys.

Then she saw Kyle and a pleasant shock rushed through her. Her attraction to him continued to puzzle her. But it didn't matter. Catty liked it.

Kyle sat alone near the enormous glass window, his head tilted in a menacing attitude. Black sunglasses hid his eyes and reflected the light from outside. That was the way Catty normally saw him—apart from everyone. Now she wondered how he'd gotten his heartbreaker's reputation. Girls talked about Kyle as if they sensed something wild inside him that they wanted to tame, but she'd never seen him with a girl, not even at Planet Bang. When he wasn't hanging out with his friends, he stood in the back, detached and glaring at everyone.

She started toward his table, her engineer's boots pounding, and wished she had worn sandals, to show off the purple polish on her toes.

A reporter wearing a wrinkled trench coat

reached Kyle first and slipped a wad of bills from his pocket into Kyle's hand. If they'd been in the school cafeteria, Catty would have thought Kyle had been selling drugs, but now she knew that he was being paid to steal information.

When the reporter walked away, Catty carried her tray over to where Kyle sat and stood next to his table, trying not to blush.

He glanced up, then kicked back the empty chair with his heavy jackboot.

She set her tray down uncertainly. Coke splashed over the edge of her paper cup, pooling on her plate.

Kyle smiled at her clumsiness, then stuffed the roll of bills into his jeans pocket.

"I'm sorry I stumbled into you." She sat, suddenly wishing she had applied some lipstick. Where had that thought come from?

Kyle stared at her, or at least she thought he did. She couldn't see his eyes, only her own reflection in the black lenses.

"So what's your interest in the manuscript?" she asked.

"Same as anyone else's." He took a French fry from his plate, doused it in ketchup, and pushed it into his mouth. "Some lucky guy buys a piece of parchment at a swap meet for fifty bucks and then sells it to the museum for millions."

"He's not so lucky," Catty reminded him. "He's dead."

Kyle nodded.

"It's curious that the papers never mentioned which swap meet he went to," Catty continued, prompting Kyle for information.

"Rose bowl, maybe," Kyle offered. "You can buy anything there."

Catty nodded, but she had gone back to last Sunday's flea market in Pasadena, spending hours in the past, walking up and down the endless rows of stalls selling new and used items, collectibles, and antiques. She hadn't seen the Scroll or the man. "I wish I knew which one."

Kyle leaned forward. "I don't think he bought the manuscript at a swap meet."

"You don't?" Catty wondered if the reporter had told Kyle something.

"It's just a cover story." He bent closer, his fingers playing over her arm.

"Why do you think that?" She glanced down at his hand, remembering his touch on her back. Then she noticed his silver ring, she had never seen a stone like the gray one set in the intricate, filigreed circle.

He pulled his hand back. "Because the person who sold the manuscript to the man hasn't come forward," Kyle answered. "And everyone is trying to find the vendor and offering big bucks for the story—you know, 'How does it feel to let a million dollars slip through your fingers?'"

"Maybe that person died, too." Catty picked up her plastic knife and fork, then started to cut her potato. She pressed too hard and the fork snapped in two, splattering oil. She grabbed a napkin and wiped her cheek, then glanced up.

Kyle's glasses were spotted with oil.

"Sorry." She handed him the napkin.

He snatched it from her, wiped the lens, then pushed back his chair. "I gotta run."

Catty picked up the potato with her fingers

and stuffed it into her mouth, watching Kyle walk away. She liked the way he carried himself, his head high, body moving slow and easy down the ramp. She wondered if he were going to break into the office now.

A reporter's loud voice, talking animatedly into his cell phone, interrupted her thoughts.

Catty's stomach tightened. No one was going to let the story about the curse die. People were too interested in the supernatural. She couldn't wait for her energy to return. She had to do something now. Maybe if she followed Kyle, she would find another entrance into the curator's office. She cleared her tray and went back outside.

She hurried down the ramp, then turned toward the Japanese gardens, pretending to study the hummingbird nests, but her eyes wandered, looking for another way in.

When she was certain no one was looking, she ducked around the side of the building next to the embankment and stopped abruptly.

Kyle stood pressed against a window, looking inside.

She stepped on a twig, and the snapping sound made him turn.

He stared at her as if she were the only one trespassing. "Are you stalking me?"

"I know you're trying to get information on the manuscript." She fumbled for words. She wanted to suggest stealing the Scroll together, but then she remembered how he had stopped her from taking it before. Maybe thievery was relative, and it was all right to steal information, but not a million-dollar artwork.

Kyle started toward her. "I'm looking at the hummingbird nests."

He stopped and boldly leaned over her. He seemed so different now from the way he had been when he had caught her stealing the Scroll. Something about him made her uneasy.

For a moment she thought he was going to kiss her, but then he whispered against her cheek, "What's *your* interest in the Scroll?"

She pulled back and stared at him in challenge. "None."

"Then you *are* stalking me," he teased.

He smiled brazenly at her and took her hand.

Catty snatched her hand away and walked off, determined not to let him see how he had affected her. When she reached the spiraling stairs, she felt foolish for running and wished she had stayed, but she wasn't going back at that point. She tried to convince herself that it didn't matter. It wasn't as if she were ever going to get a guy like Kyle, anyway. She wasn't like her friends. She didn't have their confidence with guys.

"Get over it," she whispered to herself as she climbed the steps. But she knew she couldn't.

CHAPTER SIX

ON THE BUS CATTY found a seat and settled back, the motor rumbling beneath her. At one time she had thought the evil stirrings she sometimes felt were only her imagination, but now she wondered. Her father was a member of the Atrox's Inner Circle, the Cincti, and her biological mother had been a Daughter of the Moon before becoming a Follower. How could she overcome such a birthright?

A devastating feeling of grief enveloped her. She had always thought her mother had abandoned her because she hadn't loved her enough to stay. But learning the actual reason hadn't eased the pain. Catty often speculated as to what her life would have been like if Kendra hadn't found her wandering down the highway that day. Kendra had made many sacrifices to rear Catty and keep her safe. Kendra *was* her real mother, the only one she had known, and Catty loved her dearly.

The bus pulled to the curb, swaying back and forth before it came to a stop. Catty swung her backpack over her shoulder and started toward the front. She didn't like going to Tianna's house anymore. She felt an odd presence there, as if someone were watching her. But she tried not to worry about that now. She had to get the Scroll back, and she hoped Tianna could use her telekinetic powers to help.

Catty jumped from the bus, then dodged through traffic to the other side of Wilshire Boulevard and started walking. Four blocks later she stared up at the huge Tudor house with its elaborate chimney, steeply pitched roof, and tall, narrow windows. Tianna lived there with her foster mother, Mary.

A loud thump sounded inside as Catty reached the porch. She rang the doorbell, and, moments later, footsteps hammered down the stairs.

Derek opened the door, breathless, his red hair tousled, as if he'd been in a fight. An angry welt marked his nose, and a roll of paper towels was tucked under his arm.

"What happened to you?" Catty stepped inside. She didn't have to be guarded with Derek. He knew about the Daughters.

"You'll see, soon enough." He laughed, his eyes filled with excitement. "Tianna is up in her room."

Another loud crash came from upstairs.

"What's that?" Catty followed Derek to the staircase.

"Tianna!" He started running up the steps. "She's got major pom-pom pain."

Catty took the stairs two at a time, then followed Derek into Tianna's room and stopped. She caught her breath. A book rocketed at her. She ducked, and it smashed into the wall above her. The binding broke apart, the pages fluttering to the floor.

"Sorry," Tianna yelled from the bed. Her long, silky, black hair was rolled into three snake-like coils on the back of her head and held with diamond clips. Her eyes looked red, and her fingers twitched with uncontrollable spasms.

"What happened?" Catty lunged across the bed.

"I broke my collarbone." Tianna scowled and pinched her face with discomfort.

At the same time, a glass of water slid off the nightstand and spilled onto the rug.

"The guys threw her up at an odd angle in a tumbling exercise and weren't able to catch her." Derek picked up the glass, put it back in place, then unrolled some paper towels and started sopping up the puddle.

"The fall wrecked my power," Tianna complained. "After the pain medication wore off, things started flying."

"You should have seen the hospital room." Derek tossed the wet towels in the trash.

"Do you want something to eat?" Tianna offered. "We could order pizza."

"No," Catty answered. "I came over to ask a favor, but it'll have to wait now."

"Sorry." Tianna shrugged, then flinched. "Ouch. I keep forgetting. I'll call you as soon as I'm back to normal."

Catty nodded, trying to conceal her disappointment, but she was anxious to get home. She hurried outside and started jogging. Catty had been staring up at the Hollywood sign in the hills when an odd feeling came over her. She gazed at the quiet, residential street where she lived. Tree limbs made a canopy overhead.

When she didn't see anything odd, she started walking beside a fence heavy with honeysuckle. A sudden wind gusted around her, blowing the blossoms free. She breathed the sweet fragrance, then stopped abruptly, a chill racing up her spine. The day was still. The hulking branches overhead didn't move. The leaves drooped, motionless. Her body tensed. What had caused the sudden swirl of air?

She searched for the jangle of tiny sparks that betrayed the presence of a Regulator. Not seeing any arcs of static electricity, she studied the afternoon shadows that clung to the sides of the houses and the trees.

Was it only her imagination, or had her amulet sparkled? She lifted it and looked down at the moon etched in the silver. It wasn't glowing now.

She stared back at the street, resisting the urge to run, and started walking again. Her fingers nervously played over the strap of her backpack. She forced her steps to stay slow and easy.

A few minutes later, she walked across her porch, the wind chimes silent overhead. She turned back and looked at her neighborhood. Regulators had taken up residence close to her biological mother, hoping she would lead them to Catty. Could they be living near Catty now, waiting for the Scroll to come to her again?

Farther down the street, the Stevens children played on the front lawn, their laughter trilling in the air. Jacob Passerin worked on his car, cursing, as usual. Mrs. Miller raked her lawn. Could one of them be a Regulator in disguise?

Catty unlocked her front door and hurried inside. She slid the dead bolt into place. The fragrance of clove and sandalwood incense still hung in the air. She let out a sigh, wishing her mom had been there. Kendra was away at a Reiki retreat.

In the kitchen, Catty ate Oreos and drank milk, then went upstairs and took a shower. She didn't do the homework she had put off all week. She was too tired now. She plopped onto her bed and switched on the small nightstand water fountain, hoping the sounds of flowing water would help her relax. She snuggled under a fluffy, down comforter and fell into an exhausted sleep.

Hours later, Catty awakened with a start. The fountain had been knocked over; water was dripping onto the nightstand and carpet. At first, she thought she had hit it in her sleep, but then she had the odd feeling that someone was watching her.

"Mom?" she whispered, thinking Kendra might have come home early.

When no one answered, Catty's fingers frantically searched for the flashlight she kept beside her bed for earthquake emergencies. She found it, then clicked it on and waved the beam of light around the room.

A sense of impending danger rushed over her. The room grew colder, but she saw no reason for the icy chill. Her windows were locked; the heater was on.

It wasn't the first time she had been startled awake in her bedroom. She wondered if her father came to her sometimes at night and whispered into her ear the plans he had for Catty in the future. She shuddered, thinking about him. Members of the Inner Circle were the essence of evil. Her biological mother had told her that even Regulators were afraid of her father. What would happen if Catty ever met him? Her mother had said she would meet him only when it was essential—but essential for *whom*?

CHAPTER SEVEN

MONDAY MORNING, Catty waited to go through the metal detectors in front of La Brea High. She clutched a newspaper in one hand, a cup of coffee in the other, and balanced her purse and books in the crook of her arm.

Behind her, kids danced and shouted out a new rap song. Normally she would have stopped to listen, but today she had other things on her mind.

She sipped her white-chocolate cappuccino, letting the paper cup linger on her lips, and breathed in the aroma, hoping the steam would ease the headache she had gotten after making a small jaunt back in time.

She scanned the campus, searching for Serena and Vanessa, her impatience rising. She needed to tell them about the Scroll. Maybe they could come up with a plan. If not, then perhaps it was time to tell the world the truth. Her stomach tensed.

Hi, Catty. The words tickled across her mind.

Serena stood on the front steps, waving, her cello case beside her. She wore high platform boots and a gypsy skirt.

I need to talk to you, Catty answered back, but Serena's telepathic attention had already wandered away, probably searching for Stanton.

Serena's gift had become incredibly strong since spending so much time with Stanton, but her devotion to him was dangerous, and it upset Catty. Serena was the key, the one with the power to alter the balance between light and dark, so how could she trust Stanton?

"Step on up, Catty." Mr. Bellows, one of the

security guards, interrupted her thoughts. He smiled and motioned her to his table, his gold-capped teeth catching the morning sun. He took her purse and looked inside, then rubbed his thick fingers over the material, checking for anything hidden in the lining. Last week, kids had smuggled beer onto the campus.

Catty walked through the metal detector and started across the quad. Already, heat was rising from the blacktop.

"What's up?" Serena asked, her musky perfume scenting the air. Thin gold chains of varying lengths hung from under her hair, dangling to her shoulders, each ending in a charm of moon and stars.

Catty handed Serena the newspaper clenched in her fist, but instead of reading it, Serena plunged into Catty's mind, gliding through her recent memories. Catty tried to hold back the ones of Kyle, but Serena's power was too strong.

"The Scroll?" Serena's eyes widened in disbelief. "Stanton didn't know it was back."

Catty tried to look unconcerned, but inside,

she was a whirling mix of emotions. Stanton had to have known about the Scroll. It was just one more reason Serena shouldn't see him. Catty was confident he was only using her.

"You think Stanton is playing me?" Serena looked up, her smoky eyes puzzled. "Hasn't he done enough to earn your trust yet?"

"How could Stanton not know about the Scroll?" Catty asked accusingly.

"You didn't know about it," Serena argued. "So why is he suspect?"

Catty sighed. She didn't need to fight with Serena, not now. She had more pressing problems. "It's just that he did try to take the Scroll from me, once."

Before Serena could answer, Vanessa greeted them, her smile as big as sunshine. "Hey."

"Vanessa doesn't know, either." Serena shot Catty an angry look and handed Vanessa the newspaper.

"Know what?" Vanessa began reading. Her long, surfer-blond hair was crimped today, and she wore the new, hip-hugging jeans, with the bungee cord set on the first snap, so that it pulled the waist provocatively low in front. She carried a sweater to tie around her waist before she went into class.

"The art museum has the Scroll." Catty started to sip her coffee, but her nervousness was making her nauseous, so she dropped the paper cup in a nearby trash can.

"They're translating it?" Vanessa's fingers trembled and started to blur. That was her gift. She could become invisible, but she didn't have total control over her power, especially when she was stressed. "That's big trouble. What did Chris say?"

"I haven't seen Chris." Catty didn't like the reaction visible on Vanessa's face.

"I thought Chris—" Vanessa began.

"He's supposed to protect the Scroll until he can give it to the rightful heir," Catty interrupted. "Why isn't he here to help me?"

"Like Maggie used to," Vanessa said softly and looked away. "We haven't seen her for so long. What's happening to our guides?"

Chris was more than a guide to Catty, but

she didn't want to consider what might have happened to him.

"We can't wait for Chris," Serena said. "Stanton will help us."

Catty rolled her eyes.

"What do you want us to do, then?" Serena shot back. "Go it alone against Regulators?"

"We did before," Catty answered.

"Maybe I could make the Scroll invisible," Vanessa said. "It would be easy to lift from the museum then." But her expression looked doubtful. Something big had been bothering her lately, and she'd had less control over her gift than she normally did.

"It's too dangerous," Catty warned. "I'm the only one immune to the curse."

"We don't have a choice." Vanessa handed the newspaper back to Catty and started to say more, but something distracted her.

Catty followed her look.

Tianna ran toward them, her ponytail swinging behind her. Catty was surprised to see her there at school.

"How can anyone look so gorgeous?" Serena asked, bewilderment in her voice.

"If I dressed like that—" Vanessa said, referring to Tianna's B-girl style.

"You'd still be the glamour queen," Catty interrupted, but Tianna's unearthly beauty made Catty pause. Even dressed casually in Tommy jeans and big hoop earrings, she looked incredible.

"Hi, guys." Tianna joined them on the top step.

"How's your collarbone?" Catty asked. "I didn't think you'd be able to come to school yet."

Tianna rubbed her shoulder. "Better. I can almost use my power again. At least things aren't flying around on their own anymore."

"What happened?" Vanessa asked, playing with the lace trim on her cropped camisole.

"As soon as we got back from San Diego I got hurt at cheerleading practice," Tianna told them about her fall. When she had finished, Catty handed her the paper. "We're trying to come up with a plan to get the Scroll back."

Tianna stared at the picture. Fear flashed across her face and then disappeared. She gave the paper back, her breathing harsh, as if her memory of the sorcerer Gerard de Molaire were close to the surface. He had tricked her into using the Scroll to summon the Atrox, and the curse had made her ill.

"Let's go over to the museum after school," Tianna said, even though she was obviously afraid. "It'll be easier to come up with a plan there. I can break down a wall if we need to."

"Where's Jimena?" Vanessa asked. "Maybe she can drive us over. I didn't bring my car to school. Michael drove."

"She won't be able to drive us," Serena said.

"Drive where?" Jimena pushed through the crowd of students climbing the steps and stopped next to Serena. She wore a short-sleeved, fuchsia tee that showed off the crescent-moon-and-star tattoo on her arm. Two teardrops were tattooed under her right eye, one for each of her stays in Youth Authority Camp, and a triangle of three dots adorned the web between her index finger and thumb, a reminder of when she had been ganged up and living *la vida.*

"We're going over to the art museum after school," Catty said. "Can you drive us?"

"Sorry." Jimena looked apologetic. "I've got my community-service work at Children's Hospital today." She glanced down at her wrist-watch and started to leave. "Got to go. I'll catch you later."

Her long black hair whipped behind her as she dodged through the throng of students, but then she stopped and turned back, her eyes blank with fear.

An eerie tension gathered around Catty, and in spite of the sun's warmth, her arms broke out in goose bumps.

Jimena walked back to her, kids jostling around her. "Something bad is going to happen. You feel it, don't you?"

Catty shook her head and sensed the others doing the same.

"What should we be feeling?" Serena asked.

Jimena gave Catty a quizzical look. "It's in the air, and somehow it's related to Catty." She touched the Medusa stone hanging around her neck. She no longer wore a moon amulet. She wasn't a Daughter now. On her seventeenth birthday she had chosen to give up her powers and her memories of being a goddess, but she still wore the stone given to her that last night to protect her from harm. "Be careful," she said.

Her look unnerved Catty.

"I'll be careful," Catty promised. She glanced at the small cameo pinched between Jimena's fingers.

The curling hair on the woman in the cameo was actually a nest of snakes writhing around each other. Catty watched, perplexed. The serpents' twisting had to be a trick of sunlight and shadow. She blinked, trying to sweep the image away, but the sinuous movement continued.

"Promise." Jimena touched her arm, then started easing backward, seeming unaware of the kids bumping into her.

"I promise," Catty said.

Jimena nodded, then turned and disappeared into the crush of students.

"I thought she was supposed to lose her goddess power," Serena said, as she picked up her cello case, anticipating the first bell. "But she seems more attuned to the future than ever. It's starting to freak me out."

"Maybe she was always psychic." Tianna touched the moon amulet hanging around her neck. "I had my powers before Maggie made me a Daughter."

Serena spoke in a low voice. "Have any of you noticed the way the snakes move in that cameo she wears now?"

"I wish Maggie were here," Vanessa said.

Sadness settled over them.

"I wonder what happened to her." Catty felt the loss more strongly than ever. She desperately needed to talk to Maggie and ask her what she should do.

"Maggie's dead." Serena's eyes brimmed with tears.

"Don't say that." Vanessa nudged her angrily.

"Serena's just saying what the rest of us are afraid to say," Catty added. "Only death could keep Maggie away for this long."

"Maybe she'll come back." Tianna tore off the scrunchie holding back her ponytail and shook out her hair.

Something in the tilt of Tianna's head reminded Catty of the miniature painted on the Scroll. She glanced down at the picture in the newspaper, and a chill swept through her. The resemblance between the goddess opening the jaws of hell and Tianna was uncanny. Catty slid the paper between two books, wondering if the others had noticed it.

The bell rang, and they started walking to class. Catty lingered behind.

Except for Tianna, each of the Daughters had been born a goddess. Tianna had become one, later in her life. Now, Catty wondered about her resemblance to the goddess in the picture. Could Tianna be something more than what she claimed?

CHAPTER EIGHT

THE SUN WAS ALREADY drifting toward the horizon when Catty jumped off the bus at the corner near the La Brea Tar Pits. She stopped, startled by what she saw, and Vanessa bumped into her.

Serena joined them. "What the—"

"What is it?" Tianna asked as the bus pulled away, blowing dried leaves and dust around them.

A line of people stretched from the art museum entrance down to La Brea Avenue. Street entertainers had set up an impromptu show, and the music of pipes and drums drifted toward them, adding a surreal feel to the afternoon. Yellow police tape fluttered between barriers, closing off one lane of eastbound traffic on Wilshire Boulevard, to make more room for the immense crowd.

"Do you think all these people are here to see the Scroll?" Vanessa asked, rubbing her hands together as if she were trying to stop her molecules from separating.

Tianna shook her head. "How could this many people want to see it? It's got to be a fundraiser or some special event."

"Let's go check it out." Catty started walking.

"But if this many people have come to see the Scroll, then what happens to us when they finish translating it?" Vanessa asked nervously.

"We'll be as famous as Bigfoot and the Loch Ness Monster," Serena added, increasing her pace.

Catty broke into a run. The others pounded down the sidewalk after her. The sudden smells of hot dogs and grilling onions filled the air from a stand set up in the street.

Tianna started up the steps of the museum.

"I'll get the tickets," she yelled to the others. "Get us a place in line."

Catty threaded her way through the crowd, Serena and Vanessa close behind her.

"It's like a carnival," Vanessa said.

Catty shook her head at a man offering to sell her a poster of the manuscript. Other vendors wandered up and down the sidewalk, selling T-shirts with poor renditions of the Scroll on the front and I SURVIVED THE CURSE written on the back.

A heavy woman with dozens of gold necklaces dangling from one thick arm approached them with a broad smile. "You want to buy a charm to ward off the manuscript's curse? Guaranteed to protect you."

"No, thank you," Catty said as she tried to push around her, but the woman caught her arm and pulled her back.

"What kind of charm is that around your neck?" she asked. "All sparkly and whatnot."

Catty glanced down. The intensity of her amulet's glow surprised her. "Oh, that's just the reflection from the sun," she lied and clamped her hand around it.

"I've got to get some of those," the woman said. She turned and began hawking her necklaces to others.

Catty glanced back at Vanessa. Her amulet glittered with a fiery brightness.

Vanessa slipped on her sweater, hooking the first button to hide the charm, her eyes scanning the people, looking for the danger. "Do you see anything?" she asked Catty.

"Nothing." Catty shook her head.

Serena joined them, looping a silky scarf around her neck to conceal her amulet's sparkle. "It's a full moon tonight," she began. "Followers are weakest then, but what about Regulators?"

"I don't know," Catty answered.

Tianna squeezed between a man and a woman pushing a stroller. Her hoodie was zipped over her amulet.

"The Scroll's in the special exhibition gallery. One of the guards said it would be at least an hour wait," Tianna said, and she looked around.

"I'm getting a snow cone. Anyone want anything?"

When no one answered, Tianna left them again.

"We might as well get in line." Vanessa sat down on the sidewalk next to two girls from Turney High, who were reading books on illuminated manuscripts.

Catty and Serena squeezed in on either side of Vanessa, staring at her.

"What?" Vanessa glanced down at her hands as if she feared they might have been vanishing.

"If you can make us invisible," Catty whispered, "we could get into the museum right now."

Serena clasped Vanessa's wrist, ready to go.

Vanessa shook her head. "Too many people are here. For sure, someone will see us disappear or reappear, and, with everything else going on, we don't need to add that to the mix."

Catty let her head fall back against the old May Company building that was now part of the museum complex. "You're right," she said.

An hour later, they stepped inside the

Ahmanson wing. The line circled around the open court in the middle of the building that connected all four stories. Abruptly, the air shifted, becoming cold and unnaturally heavy.

The two girls in front of Catty giggled and waved their hands over their heads.

"Do you feel it?" Tianna whispered.

Serena nodded. "Who wouldn't?"

Catty rubbed her temples, wondering why she felt suddenly so dizzy. She was supposed to be immune to the Scroll's curse. Then, with a jolt, she realized that the power coming from the parchment was pulsing gently around her, seeping into her lungs, not threatening but caressing her in welcome, its force stronger than ever.

"It didn't feel like this before, did it?" Catty asked, certain that it hadn't.

Vanessa shook her head, trying to mask her fear, but Catty had known her long enough to see through her guise.

Catty glanced at Serena, and by her vacant gaze, knew she was sending out her thoughts, searching for Regulators.

"I can barely breathe," Tianna whispered.

Catty looked at the people surrounding them. "Why isn't everyone afraid?" she asked.

"They think the museum is creating the hype around the Scroll to get more visitors," Serena answered with authority, her eyes still wide and focused on something only she could see. "No one believes there's really a curse. They just think the odd vibration coming from the Scroll is a special effect created by the curators."

"That's why they're acting like this is some kind of haunted house." Tianna started to shiver, then pulled the hood of her sweatshirt over her head against the cold.

Catty wondered if the Scroll had become that powerful, but before she could consider further, a different sensation rolled over her in waves. It was an unmistakable electrical charge.

A jagged, blue bolt crackled overhead. It looked like tiny, forked lightning. It hung over Catty for a moment before twisting back with a dreadful snap.

The two girls in front of her jumped and

tried to catch the sparks cascading to the floor. Other people squealed with delight; no one seemed panicked.

"The Regulators have found us! Where are they?" Catty asked impatiently. Instinct told her to run, but she walked cautiously forward, her body tense.

"Close," Serena muttered, her face tight with concentration as her mind continued to explore.

"The Scroll must be able to affect people even through the display case," Vanessa said. "I feel feverish."

Serena nudged Catty's elbow. "Regulators," she whispered. "I found them."

Catty's head snapped around, frantically studying the faces in the crowd.

When the line moved forward, closer to the display, Vanessa pointed, and at the same moment, the odd electrical vibration grew stronger, seizing Catty and pulsing through her.

Three tall men with silky, gray hair and perfectly fitted black suits stood in front of a display of pre-Columbian art.

"They look like escapees from a wax museum," Tianna said.

Vanessa grasped Catty's arm as if she needed an anchor. Catty could feel the buzz of Vanessa's molecules trying to break free from gravity.

Tianna foled her arms over her chest. "I wonder what they look like without their disguise."

"You don't want to see." Catty shuddered, remembering other encounters.

"We'll beat them." Vanessa spoke confidently. "Just because they're powerful doesn't mean they're smart."

"At least they can't destroy the Scroll," Serena said to Catty. "Only you can do that."

"But if they can get it first, they could take it away and make it impossible for us to find." Catty's sense of urgency grew, but it wasn't just the Regulators that concerned her. She didn't like the way people seemed to be affected by the Scroll's curse so quickly. She stared at the illuminated manuscript displayed inside the circular case. She would have felt overcome by its beauty if the smell of menthol cough drops hadn't been so strong. Coughs echoed around her, some deep and guttural.

A woman sneezed on the glass and the people with her laughed, but their own eyes looked red and puffy with fever. Did they think their physical symptoms were also special effects?

She turned to Serena.

"They don't get it," Serena answered her mental question. "It's as if the Scroll has given them a sense of euphoria to keep them from worrying about how sick they're becoming."

"We have to act quickly," Catty said.

"When?" Vanessa asked.

"Tonight," Catty answered, as a heavy foreboding settled over her.

CHAPTER NINE

CATTY WALKED THROUGH the park behind the museum. A late afternoon breeze rushed through the trees, stirring leaves. Vanessa, Serena, and Tianna had gone over to The Grove to eat dim sum at Madame Woo's, but Catty's stomach was churning and the thought of food made her queasy. Her mind raced, trying to find another way to get the Scroll without exposing her friends to its curse or to the Regulators.

Her concern quickly turned to self-reproach. If she had stolen the Scroll when she'd had the chance, no one would have been in danger now. She considered going back in time for one last try, but she was too concerned that if she did, she would use up her remaining energy, and she might need it in the coming hours.

Catty turned down another path, the late afternoon shadows stretching in front of her. When she glanced up, she saw Kyle sitting on a bench, his back to her, wearing jeans and a faded black T-shirt, wind ruffling his hair. A drawing pad rested on his knee and a tackle box filled with pencils and charcoals sat beside him.

Curiosity got the best of her. She crept up behind him, avoiding dried leaves and twigs that might have given her away. Then, from a safe distance, she watched him sketch a boy and a dog playing catch with a Frisbee.

His hand darted to the top of the page to draw in the clouds, and his spiked, leather bracelet caught the sun.

Her eyes drifted up his chest and neck to his profile. Even with most of his face turned from her, she could see that he was incredibly handsome, and before she could repress her thoughts, her mind filled with the memory of his body pressed against hers.

"Hi, Catty," Kyle said without turning.

She caught her breath. "How did you—" and then she saw her shadow stretching over the bench and onto the grass in front of him. But a shadow didn't have detail. "You couldn't have known it was me," she argued.

"I recognized your scent," he answered without looking at her.

She laughed nervously and in spite of herself sniffed under her arms.

His laughter made her stop. He was still watching her shadow. Her face burned. Had he seen her?

"Your scented shampoo," he said. "Or maybe it's a body lotion, I don't know. I like it."

"Shampoo," she answered, hoping he wouldn't turn now and see her blush.

"You've been standing there for at least ten minutes." He flipped the sketch pad closed. "I was waiting for you to say something."

"You're really talented," she said, hoping to change the subject. She had no explanation for what she had been doing. "I don't have that kind of imagination."

"You do," he said, and turned. "I've seen your work."

"Thank you." She blushed again, her eyes suddenly nervous and afraid to look into his. She became self-conscious of the low-cut waistline of her jeans. She ran a nervous finger across her exposed hip bone and bit her lip. What was happening to her?

"If you're so interested in my drawing, maybe you'd like to see my paintings." He picked up his pad, snapped the tackle box shut, and started walking toward the parking lot. "Coming?"

She wanted to see his work, but that meant spending time with him, and she had other things she needed to do. She glanced up as he disappeared behind a hedge. She sighed heavily, undecided, then ran after him, hating the way he made her feel confused and uneasy. She stopped at the edge of the parking lot.

He stood beside the passenger-side door of an old, rusted Chevy, waiting for her. She scowled. How had he known she would follow him? His conceit was unbearable. Catty thought she probably disliked him more than any guy she had ever met.

He chuckled. "Did something upset you?"

"No," she said.

He opened the door of his car and she slid in. The interior smelled of stale beer and cigarettes. Gently he eased the door closed, still smiling at her.

The sun had set by the time they drove under the gold dragon archway and entered the streets of Chinatown. A fanfare of neon lights and spicy fragrances filled the car. Catty rolled her window down. "You live here?"

"In a loft at the other end. They just converted the old mill into apartments. I get free rent in exchange for maintenance."

Catty studied him. "You live alone?"

"With friends," he answered vaguely.

Minutes later, Catty walked slowly into the

huge room, her footsteps echoing. A streetlight cast an amber glow across the unfinished floor. Drop cloths and easels, paints, palettes, and sketch pads cluttered long tables.

Kyle opened a window, and an incredible smell filled the air. "That's the barbecued pork buns from downstairs," he said. "They're killer. Want to try some?"

"Another time," Catty said, wondering why he didn't turn on the lights. "I have something I have to do tonight."

A match flared, and Kyle began lighting an array of candles set about the room. He smiled sheepishly in the firelight. "I forgot to pay the electric bill."

Catty walked to the other side of the room. Even in the dim lighting she could see the huge canvases. The flickering flames seemed to make the surreal landscapes come alive. "I've never seen places like this," she said, as she gestured toward one of the paintings. "Do you think they really exist?"

"Yes," he whispered.

She could feel him watching her, and then his footsteps sounded on the floor, and she sensed him close behind her.

"I like this one," Catty said and paused, amazed at the daring simplicity of the seascape, though the vastness of sky and ocean filled her with an intense loneliness. "I think I've seen this beach. Is it nearby?"

"Very close."

His hand brushed against her bare waist and guided her to the next canvas. The painting disturbed her. It showed only a line of trees, and there was something terrifying about it, the colors dark and brooding. Still, it looked so familiar, like something she remembered from a dream.

"*Dark Hides the Night,*" he whispered from behind her, his breath rushing down her neck. "That's what I call this one."

Her throat tightened with nerves.

Then his hand shot out, his finger outlining a shadow hovering in the branches.

She bit her lip to keep from leaning against

his arm. He drew his hand back and let it rest lightly on her shoulder. His touch made her breath catch.

"This is really great work," she said, trying to keep her voice steady.

"Do you like it?"

"Yes." She closed her eyes, feeling his chest brush against her back.

Then, before she was even aware of what she was doing, she turned, wrapped her arms around him, and pressed her body against his.

She glanced up at him and boldly slipped her hands up his back. She wanted his kiss. If he pushed her away now, she didn't know what she'd do. But he smiled, his arms encircled her, and his fingers brushed the bare skin above her jeans. He looked down at her, taking his time and making her hungry with anticipation, and then his lips touched hers, surprisingly soft and warm.

A jolt of pleasure rushed through her.

She started to panic. How could she have been so brazen?

But his kiss, so slow and tender, made her

forget her worries. He kissed her again, and this time she had the odd sensation that something was pulling energy from her. Her strength slipped through her veins, spiraling away. She felt drained. Was Kyle doing something to her?

Suddenly, his hands stopped searching, and he pulled back, startling her. "I'm sorry, Catty. I'd better take you home."

"What?" she asked, feeling robbed. She stumbled backward, the room spinning, and nearly fell.

Kyle grabbed her arm. "Are you okay, Catty?"

She blinked. She'd only kissed one other guy before. She glanced up at Kyle, her cheeks warm. Had her kiss been that bad?

"Come on." He started walking around the room, pinching out candle flames. The smell of smoke filled the air, and then he came back to her, slipped his arm around her shoulder, and started walking her to the door.

After a few failed attempts at conversation, they drove back to her house in silence. She climbed out of the car and slammed the door. She didn't bother to say good-bye. She was never going to see Kyle again, anyway, and if she hadn't been so exhausted she'd have gone into the past and stolen back her kiss then and there. That was a definite "to do" for later. No way was he keeping a memory of this evening so he could laugh about her kisses with his friends.

CHAPTER TEN

IT WAS ALMOST EIGHT when the horn honked. Catty hurried down the stairs, tying the belt of her wrap sweater, and ran outside.

Vanessa was parked at the curb in her 1965 red Mustang convertible, her hair frosted with silver streaks. Catty slid into the front seat.

"Ready?" Vanessa asked. She wore a bell-sleeved sweater and matching purple mascara.

"Let me borrow your makeup." Catty reached for Vanessa's purse from the back and pulled out the makeup bag. "If we're caught tonight, I want to look good for my mug shot."

Vanessa laughed, her tense mood broken, and she pulled away from the curb as Catty swept electric-blue liner over her lids.

"I just burned a new CD." Vanessa punched a button on her newly installed stereo, and guitar music roared into the night. Vanessa's voice flowed from the speakers, a magical blend of rock and soul.

"That's really good," Catty said, complimenting her, and she spread red gloss over her lips. She turned to face Vanessa. "What do you think?"

"You look like a vamp and totally smoochable."

Catty hesitated, wondering if she should tell Vanessa about Kyle. But before she could find the words, the car headlights swept over the shadows in Serena's front yard, and they pulled over to the curb. Automatically, Catty searched the dark for moving shadows, wondering if Stanton were near.

Serena waved from the front door and ran out to the car, pulling a fluffy hooded sweater over her velvet tank top. Rhinestones sparkled in her hair.

"I think she's seeing too much of Stanton," Vanessa whispered to Catty as Serena approached.

Vanessa spent time with Michael and his band, rehearsing and performing, but she also made time for the Daughters. Serena didn't.

"What do they do together? She never talks about it anymore," Catty said in a low tone.

Serena jumped into the backseat, her perfume enveloping them. "Hey," she said. "I'm so ready for this. It feels like forever since we've done anything together."

"It's been a long time," Vanessa agreed, looking pointedly at Catty.

Serena leaned forward. "Let's not get into it tonight," she whispered, as if she had caught their thoughts. "I promise, you guys are still my priority."

Catty nodded. "We miss you. That's all."

Vanessa punched a button to skip to the next song. As the beat vibrated through them, they danced with their hands, their upper bodies moving, wind blowing through their hair.

By the time they pulled up in front of the

large Tudor house, Tianna was already waiting for them outside in a slinky jumpsuit, a chain belt slung around her hips.

"Hey, guys." She jumped in next to Serena.

A song and a half later, Vanessa shut off the music and parked on a side street near the museum.

"Ready?" Vanessa opened her car door, got out, and stepped under a tree.

Silently, they joined her, each lost in her own thoughts. A sudden breeze raced through the leaves, whipping shadows around them.

"No negative thoughts or doubts," Vanessa cautioned as they clasped hands, forming a chain.

Catty tried to give Vanessa a reassuring smile, but her own lips seemed frozen.

Vanessa's eyes widened, a golden aura shimmered around her, and her power began to build. Immediately, Catty felt energy burn beneath her skin. Her molecules became restless, and her muscles stretched, pulling on bone. She gasped at the pain, but soon the discomfort dulled to a gentle ache.

Vanessa's face blurred, fluttering into a swarm of specks before she disappeared.

Catty floated up over the trees, the full moon's light washing over her. She loved the sensation of flying, of rippling through the air. Her senses seemed more vibrant now. She could taste the night, the tinge of ocean in the breeze, and even the sweet fragrance from a honeysuckle bush far below.

Vanessa guided them, as they curled sinuously down through the locked gate at the front entrance to the museum; then they rode a sudden gust up high, skimming the skylights over the plaza.

Security guards wandered back and forth far below them, their footsteps resonating through the space.

"Ready?" Vanessa whispered, her voice no more than a sigh of wind.

Their speed increased, the buildings whizzing by as they jetted down, risking their lives if Vanessa didn't stop in time. In seconds, they were only inches from the concrete. Sudden dizziness overcame Catty. She screamed, but her shriek came out a wheeze.

Abruptly, Vanessa turned. They passed under a crack beneath the doors and skidded along the floor, their molecules mixing with dust.

Vanessa swirled up in a lazy spiral and released them. They floated down, landing feet first on the floor, their bodies translucent and shimmering.

Immediately Catty felt the presence of the Scroll. Its force settled over her, making her molecules collide. She grimaced, then took a deep breath, trying to calm her hammering heart.

Vanessa became solid, an odd look on her face.

Hurrying footsteps sounded, coming closer, as Serena and Tianna became solid again.

A burly guard rounded the corner, his eyes alert.

"Hey," he shouted, alarm crossing his face. "How did you girls get in here?"

Serena quickly used her mind control to stop

the guard. A dreamy smile crossed his jowly face, and he appeared to fall asleep standing up.

"What did you do?" Catty asked.

"I pulled sleep forward with a good dream," Serena explained. "He'll stay that way for a few minutes at least."

"I'll break the glass," Tianna said, her pupils dilating with energy.

"Wait." Catty touched her. "It'll make too much noise. Let Vanessa go inside and bring the Scroll back out."

"It's probably airtight," Tianna argued, anxious to use her power.

"I'll try." Vanessa elongated her body, becoming a series of thin threads stretching high into the air and then vanishing.

A hissing sound followed, and the Scroll flapped as if something had disturbed it.

"Vanessa's in the display case," Catty whispered, and she looked around, fearing the approach of another guard but more afraid of what the Scroll's curse might do to Vanessa.

Without warning, an ear-piercing scream

shattered the silence, and Vanessa smashed back together, becoming visible inside the display case, her legs and arms at odd angles, a startled look on her face.

An alarm went off, and footsteps echoed throughout the building.

"What happened?" Catty pressed her hands against the glass, feeling an odd vibration emanating from the Scroll.

"It sucked my energy away." Vanessa gasped. She seemed to be having a difficult time breathing.

"Make yourself invisible," Catty urged. "The guards are coming."

"I can't!" Vanessa yelled. "I'm trapped."

CHAPTER ELEVEN

CATTY STOOD WITH her hands pressed on the glass, staring at Vanessa imprisoned in the display case. Already her appearance had changed. Her skin looked pallid and coarse, deep bluish circles had developed around her eyes, and labored breaths rasped from her lungs.

"Hurry," Catty said, glancing back at Tianna.

"I'm trying." Tianna strained, her hands clenched and trembling.

A nearby bench rocked back and forth, then streaked across the floor, speeding past them before it crashed into the wall with a thundering boom. Plaster and dust sprayed out from the impact.

"I'm still messed up!" Tianna exclaimed. An odd glow whirled around her as her energy field continued to build without direction.

"Duck!" Serena screamed.

An air-conditioning grille tore from the ceiling and catapulted toward Catty. She dodged, and it whizzed by, grazing her cheek, before hitting the floor and clattering noisily to a stop.

"Sorry." A sheepish grin crossed Tianna's face.

"Try again," Catty cried as she ran to Tianna, hoping to fortify her friend's strength with her own. Their hands locked, and immediately Catty's power began draining into Tianna.

"We've got company!" Serena shouted.

A huge guard rounded the corner and stopped, a whistle escaping his mouth. "What are you girls—" Then his eyes shifted from Vanessa to the bench impaled in the wall and back to the first guard Serena had entranced with slumber.

Vanessa clawed at the glass, her hands going

in and out of focus, stark terror in her eyes. "Catty!"

A female guard collided with the watchman, then peered past his huge stomach and looked into the room, her eyes widening as she stared dumbfounded at Vanessa. She crept forward, awestruck. "What in the world?"

"The curse," the watchman whispered behind her, his voice haunted. "Must be the curse." He pulled out his gun and stepped forward, his hands shaking, the barrel pointed at Vanessa.

Catty's heartbeat quickened. "Do something, Serena."

"I'm trying." Serena's tongue ring clicked nervously against her teeth; her pupils grew large.

Suddenly the two guards became still, chins falling, heads nodding, as slumber claimed them. The watchman's gun fell to the floor with a loud thump.

Relief flooded through Catty.

"Hurry," Serena warned. "I can't control all three of them for long."

Tianna squinted in concentration. When her

eyes opened, a fiery light crackled across the room and hit the display case. The glass exploded with a loud blast, and shards came flying out.

Vanessa tumbled to the ground with a startled cry, clutching the Scroll.

Catty rushed to her, her soles crunching over shattered glass, and helped her to stand.

Without warning, all three guards awakened from their trance.

"I lost them!" Serena shouted. "The noise startled me."

"What now?" Tianna stepped backward.

"I erased their memories of seeing Vanessa in the display case," Serena continued in a panicked voice. "But now, they think we're thieves who have broken into the museum to steal the Scroll."

Simultaneously, the heavy guard lifted his hand and yelled, "Freeze!"

An odd look crossed his face. His pudgy hand was empty, the gun no longer clutched in his palm. He looked around till he saw it, then gingerly grabbed it from the floor and held it at point-blank range, and aimed at them.

"Somebody do something," Tianna said. A shard of glass trembled beneath her feet. "My power's too wacko to even try."

"Don't look at me." Vanessa rasped. "I can barely stand."

Serena glanced at the Scroll in Vanessa's hands. "Maybe the curse is doing something."

"It's draining us," Vanessa agreed. "Open the tunnel, Catty."

"So that's how you got in here," the guard said. "Where's the tunnel?"

"Let me see what I can do," Catty said.

"Don't try anything," the female guard warned, approaching with handcuffs. She reached for Catty's hand, but when their fingers touched, the guard jerked back as if she had been shocked.

A tremendous torrent of energy surged inside Catty, making the fine hairs on the back of her neck rise.

The woman looked up, startled, feeling the change in the air. The man holding the gun stepped closer.

"He won't shoot," Serena whispered. "I caught his thoughts."

A black opening appeared in the air, hovering behind Catty.

"What is it?" the woman gasped and stepped back, the handcuffs clattering to the ground.

"Bye-bye." Catty smirked and grabbed Vanessa's hand.

Serena whooped and Tianna laughed as they lunged forward and grabbed on to Catty.

An unnaturally bright light flooded the room, and the guards lifted their arms to shield their eyes from the glare.

But as Catty was sucked into the widening black hole, the woman guard sprinted forward and caught her leg.

Catty shrieked, tumbling to the ground, and Vanessa, Serena, and Tianna fell after her. The tunnel closed with a tremendous roar, whipping up the air around them and leaving them trapped in the present.

Catty scrambled to her feet.

"What are we going to do now?" Vanessa asked.

"Our number one backup plan," Catty yelled. "Run!" She grabbed Vanessa's hand and darted away, pulling her along.

Serena and Tianna sprinted after them.

The piercing sound of alarms grew louder as they approached the stairwell.

They started down the steps, stumbling in the dim light. The Scroll fell from Vanessa's hand. She turned and started back after it, but the guards were already at the top of the stairs.

"Leave it!" Catty ran up to Vanessa, yanked her wrist and pulled her away.

On the lower level, they slipped into a special art exhibition of mummy cases and slid behind a row of dried-out bodies exposed beneath layers of bandages and resin.

"Couldn't you have chosen a better place to hide?" Vanessa whispered, closing her eyes.

A dry whistle escaped Serena. Catty glanced up.

The stout guard entered the room, his flashlight beam sweeping over a sarcophagus.

"I know you can make us invisible," Catty

said, encouraging Vanessa. "Just follow your own advice. No negative thoughts. Picture where you want to go."

Vanessa closed her eyes, and a gentle radiance spilled from her, circling Catty, its tendrils spreading out and curling around Serena and Tianna.

"Hey," the guard shouted. "I found them."

Vanessa's face remained placid, and her power continued flowing. Catty's hands blurred, then stretched, fluttering into a mist as she evaporated.

The guard staggered backward. His flashlight hit the doorjamb with a loud *thwack.*

Catty disappeared and floated over him, as Vanessa guided her, Serena, and Tianna. They swirled into the central courtyard, then rose to the first floor.

When they approached the entrance, Catty felt Vanessa's struggle to keep them invisible. What would happen if they materialized and became wedged under the door? Catty tried to push the thought away.

Vanessa dived, pulling them into a thin

thread, then whipped through a crack between the doors and whirled up into the night, spiraling over the Anderson Building, the full moon's radiance gleaming through them, with silver kisses.

When they neared Wilshire Boulevard, a black cloud rushed over the face of the moon, and they plunged to the ground, their molecules slamming together. Catty hit the sidewalk and skidded along the concrete, scraping her palms. She lay still, exhausted, trying to catch her breath.

"We've got to get out of here," Catty said, her lips brushing against the grimy sidewalk, but she didn't move. Her arms and legs felt too shaky for her to stand.

Catty had combined energies with Tianna before without losing her own strength, so why did she feel so weak this time? Her mind kept flashing back to Kyle. Had his kiss really stolen some of her power? Maybe she had just exhausted her strength. "How could everything go so terribly wrong?" she asked.

Serena stood slowly, stretching out her back.

Distant sirens filled the air, becoming louder

than the alarms that still vibrated inside the museum.

"We're never going to be able to explain what we were doing." Vanessa shuddered, her eyes brimming with tears.

"They'll never catch us." Tianna brushed off her jumpsuit. "No one will believe the surveillance tapes are real."

Vanessa looked up. "How did the helicopters get here so quickly?"

The thumping vibration of rotating blades roared over them.

"We'd better go." Catty pulled herself up and started limping across Wilshire Boulevard.

"Look out!" Vanessa screamed behind her.

Catty turned and froze. A car blasted toward her, headlights shining, horn blaring.

CHAPTER TWELVE

THE CAR SKIDDED around Catty and jerked to a stop, its engine rumbling. Immediately, Catty recognized the '81 blue-and-white Oldsmobile. Jimena sat in the driver's seat, her eyes darting nervously back and forth, scanning the street.

"Get in," Jimena shouted over the thundering music.

Catty opened the door and jumped into the front. Vanessa, Tianna, and Serena tumbled into the back.

Before they could even slam the doors, Jimena jammed her foot on the accelerator. The tires spun with a terrible squeal, filling the air with the acrid smell of burning rubber. At once the Olds screeched away, setting off antitheft alarms in the cars parked along Wilshire Boulevard.

"Why are you here?" Catty asked, snapping her seat belt into place. She glanced back at the others, their hair whipping wildly around their faces. They appeared as bewildered as she felt.

"I knew I had to come save your butts. What have you been up to?" Jimena asked over the heavy beat of an old rap song.

"But how did you know to come here?" Serena asked. "Were you just driving in the neighborhood?"

Jimena's fingers curled tighter around the steering wheel, and she stared at Catty. "Intuition," she said, her tone daring Catty to contradict her.

"The road!" Vanessa squealed from behind.

Jimena and Catty turned back toward the windshield. A galaxy of red brake lights glared in front of them.

Catty sucked in air, then swayed against her

seat belt as the car dodged around the slowing traffic.

Vanessa leaned forward. "Maybe we could slow down a bit, too."

"Who's the one who's escaped cops before?" Jimena shot back. "You or me?"

Vanessa settled into her seat. "Just don't ever comment on my driving again."

Jimena laughed and pressed her hand hard on the horn. "We're going through."

"The light's red," Catty warned.

"You think I don't know that?" Jimena asked.

The car blasted into the intersection, narrowly missing a Cadillac, then spun around a truck loaded with pipes. Horns blared. Cars swerved and braked.

"We're going to crash!" Vanessa yelled.

Jimena hunched over the steering wheel, eyes frozen in concentration, and zipped around a Jaguar.

Catty felt a change in the air and turned to peek at the backseat. Serena put her arm around Vanessa and held her tightly, cautioning her.

Vanessa's face was dissolving, and the Daughters couldn't let Jimena see that anymore.

"What were you doing in the museum, anyway?" Jimena asked.

"Nothing, really," Catty lied.

"I went to jail twice for doing nothing." Jimena slammed on the brakes.

Catty's head wrenched backward.

The car spun around the next corner. Then Jimena switched off the headlights, pulled into a driveway, and killed the engine.

"Heads down," she warned and ducked her head under the steering wheel.

Catty rolled beneath the dashboard, her heart hammering. The car became eerily quiet except for Vanessa's rattling breaths.

A beam of moonlight fell on Jimena's face. Catty saw her eyes glistening and had the oddest sensation that Jimena was about to cry.

"What?" Catty whispered.

"Nada." Jimena shook her head and caught the tears sliding down her cheeks with the side of her hand.

The tears surprised Catty. Jimena had been in a gang, jacking cars and worse, before she discovered her true destiny. Nothing ever bothered her. Another thought came to Catty. When Jimena had her goddess powers she had always been forewarned when something bad was going to happen. Now Catty wondered if Jimena had seen something in the future—something worse than the trouble at the museum.

"Are you okay?" Catty asked, as she rubbed Jimena's hand, surprised to find the skin cold and sticky.

Jimena put a finger to her lips, silencing her.

At the same moment, helicopter blades stirred the air, sweeping tree branches back and forth and spinning shadows inside the car.

Silence followed, the seconds stretching into minutes.

At last, Jimena sat up and turned the key in the ignition. The engine rumbled gently as she backed from the drive.

Catty took her place, buckling herself in with a sharp click of metal.

Serena rested her chin on the seat back between Catty and Jimena. "Now tell us how you knew we needed help."

"I'm not sure." Jimena drove down a residential street toward Burton Way. "It started this afternoon at the hospital. The idea popped into my head and kept getting stronger. By the time I got home I was shaking. *Mi abuelita* told me to trust my intuition and gave me the keys to my brother's car." Jimena shrugged and glanced at Serena in the rearview mirror. "So, here I am. Now, you tell me. What were you doing?"

"We were trying to get a look at the manuscript," Serena lied. "You know, the one everyone is talking about."

"We peeked through the glass doors in the front," Vanessa added nervously. "How were we to know alarms would go off?"

"Is that right?" Jimena fixed her gaze on Catty. "How did you get past the locked gates?"

"They weren't locked in back." Catty looked away, hating to lie to Jimena. They had been through too much together.

Jimena jammed on the brakes.

Catty turned back, startled.

Anger flashed in Jimena's eyes. "I know you're lying to me."

"We'd tell you the truth if we could." Serena sounded distressed. Of all the Daughters, she had been closest to Jimena.

"You'd tell me if you were my friends," Jimena said, her lips quivering. "Get out, all of you."

Catty reluctantly climbed out into the street in front of the Beverly Center. Tianna, Vanessa, and Serena joined her on the sidewalk.

Jimena eased back into traffic and drove away without waving good-bye.

"She's really been weird lately," Serena said. "Maybe we should tell her the truth."

Catty shook her head. "We can't. Didn't you go in her mind and check out her thoughts?"

"I couldn't get inside," Serena admitted.

"What do you mean?" Tianna brushed her hands through her hair, sending tiny pieces of glass to the sidewalk.

"Her thoughts are protected," Serena explained. "By a really strong power."

"You don't need to be a mind reader to know she's keeping something from us," Vanessa added with a heavy sigh.

"But how does she have the power to keep her thoughts from Serena?" Catty asked.

CHAPTER THIRTEEN

CATTY AWAKENED WITH a start, a blinding shaft of sunlight in her eyes. The pencils and paintbrushes on her desk clattered against each other, and she jerked up, thinking, *Earthquake.*

At the same time, the air shimmered, undulating into a hazy apparition, and Vanessa materialized, wearing a low-slung skirt with side slits and carrying a newspaper rolled in one hand.

"Give it up, Vanessa." Catty fell back on her pillow. "I'm not going to school today." But as she yanked the covers over her head, she glimpsed her clock radio. It read eleven o'clock. She sprang up, jarring the headboard, and swung her legs over the side of the bed, a sheet tangled around her ankle. "It's fourth period. Why aren't you at school?"

"I skipped." Vanessa's face flushed. "Read this!" She thrust the paper at Catty. "I saw it on Mr. Darston's desk."

"You stole his paper?" Catty opened *The L.A. Times,* impressed. Vanessa never broke the rules.

"He won't miss it." Vanessa brushed her trembling hands through her hair. "Someone stole the Scroll last night."

"Do they mention us?" Catty didn't wait for an answer but started reading.

"Like the guards would ever admit what they saw us do." Vanessa flung herself onto the bed and kicked off her ankle boots, her toenails flashing ruby colors.

"But the police must have seen us on the surveillance tapes." Catty imagined a fuzzy, black-and-white image of her face broadcast on the nightly news.

"I know." Vanessa ran a finger over the print, the stone on her mood ring black. "But it says the police have no clues. Exploding glass destroyed the cameras in the exhibit room, and the images on the videotapes were too blurred for identification."

Catty felt giddy with relief, but then she thought about the missing manuscript, and her chest tightened. "Regulators must have taken it."

"That's what I figured, too."

"They must have been following us." Catty stared at the ceiling, trying to concentrate on recovering the Scroll, but her thoughts kept turning to Kyle. She sighed. "I'm becoming obsessed."

"What?" Vanessa rolled closer to her, "'Fess up. What haven't you been telling me?"

A blush warmed Catty's face.

"What?" Vanessa demanded. "You can't say something like that and not give me the details."

"Do you remember Kyle Ormond?" Catty asked.

"That lo—" Vanessa stopped, her lips frozen in a pucker.

Catty walked over to her desk, picked up a sketch pad and pencil, and began drawing Vanessa, trying to capture the way the light fell on her face. "You were going to say *loser*," Catty said at last.

"All right. I was," Vanessa answered, trying to remain still for Catty. "He's got to-die-for looks, but his reputation—"

"I know, but I'm crushing on him, anyway." Catty made quick pencil strokes across the paper and slowly began to tell Vanessa about meeting Kyle.

By the time she had finished, the portrait was done, and the sun had disappeared behind an oak tree. A pattern of leaves and branches shadowed the bedroom.

"Maybe you just miss Chris," Vanessa suggested.

"I do miss Chris, but what I feel for Kyle is different . . . it's like my emotions are raw." She paused, wishing she could explain the way her insides went on a rampage every time she saw Kyle. She tossed her sketch pad aside. "How can

I lust after this guy when we have to get the Scroll back? I can't get him out of my mind."

"Nothing stops me from thinking about Michael," Vanessa said, her eyes dreamy.

"But, I mean, I'm thinking about . . . you know?" Catty patted her cheeks, trying to keep the heat from rising to them.

"Of course I think about that." Vanessa stood and grabbed the blue fingernail polish from Catty's dresser. "Let's forget about the Scroll for now and pretend we're just normal girls with regular problems."

Catty chewed on the end of her pencil. "I wish it were that simple."

"Me, too," Vanessa said, shaking a bottle of nail polish. "You're going to Planet Bang tonight, aren't you? I'm going to sing with Michael's band tonight."

"I don't know," Catty said. "If I go there, I'll probably run into Kyle."

Vanessa grabbed Catty's hand and started brushing polish over her nails. The acetone smell filled the air. "That's a good reason for going."

* * *

That night, Catty stared at her reflection in her dressing-table mirror and carefully placed stick-on crystals around her ears, one above the other, then slipped dangling drop earrings into the holes in her lobes.

She took a metallic-blue eyeliner and drew delicate, swirling designs on her hands and a matching motif around her belly button. Next, she dusted sparkling powder over her skin to set the makeup, then eased into a low-cut mini and a cropped top the color of the sky. She wanted to look totally goddess tonight.

When Catty arrived at Planet Bang, Vanessa was on stage singing, the smoky mists roiling around her and flashing with laser lights. Catty could feel the sadness in the lyrics. She searched the crowd looking for her other friends.

Tianna danced with Derek, her hands lifted over her head. Her hips moved sensuously under the drape of her clinging skirt. Derek had wrapped his hands around her waist, and when she lifted her head, he kissed her cheek.

Sudden, burning jealousy overpowered Catty. She wished she were dancing with Kyle. She glanced toward the back, hoping to see him, but instead saw Serena, standing next to Jimena, in a lacy halter top and hot-pink flares, her bare back glimmering with glitter.

Catty jostled through the dancers and joined them.

"I tried to call you earlier." Silvery white shadow lined Serena's eyes, and her hair fell in sexy spirals. "Did you see the paper?"

Catty nodded.

"What about the paper?" Jimena wore an off-the-shoulder satin top, her hip bones jutting over the low-cut waist of her sparkling, purple slacks. She seemed to have forgotten her anger of the previous night.

Before Catty could answer, Ollie asked Jimena to dance. He played in the school orchestra. He towered over her. His movements were awkward, but Jimena didn't mind. She laughed when he stepped on her foot.

"Where's Collin?" Catty asked Serena.

"Hawaii again. He's so into surfing. I don't know how Jimena can put up with it."

Then Serena changed the subject. "Should I ask Stanton what he knows about the Scroll?"

Catty bit her lip.

"Don't bother to say it." Serena folded her arms across her chest. "I caught your thoughts."

"It's just that we can't—"

"Trust him?" Serena finished the sentence, but then she hung her arm around Catty, and her tone softened. "I like Stanton in spite of what you think of him. The same way you like Kyle in spite of his bad-boy reputation. So, maybe you'd like Stanton if you took the time to know him."

"How did you find out about Kyle?" Catty asked, giving her a look. "You know I hate it when you snoop around my mind."

"It's not like I was prying," Serena answered. "Kyle's name is practically written on your brain. You *lo-o-ove* him!" she teased.

"I don't even like him," Catty snapped.

Serena smirked. "I guess I know your feelings better than you do."

"Besides," Catty went on. "There's a big difference between Kyle and Stanton. Stanton—"

"And I can feel him calling me. See you later." Serena left Catty and hurried to the back of the room.

An unnatural shadow formed in the corner, whirling into a gauzy vapor before becoming a swaying, black shape. Serena stepped into the velvet darkness, and Stanton formed beside her, embracing her. His spiky, blond hair made him look like any other high school guy. He kissed Serena's temple, and she leaned against him, caressing his hands; then they dissolved into a misty silhouette and disappeared.

The song ended, and the drummer took up a slow tempo. Michael started playing the guitar, his fingers running up and down the neck. The energy in the room changed, and Vanessa began to sing a soulful melody for lovers. The haunting sound filled Catty with yearning.

Couples took to the dance floor, snuggling against each other. Catty watched, remembering how long it had been since she had danced with a guy she really liked.

Jimena joined her. "*¿Que te pasa?* You look like you need a friend."

"I think I'm going to barf." Catty's stomach cramped with bitter envy. She studied Jimena, wondering how she had gotten over her anger so easily.

"This place is dead." Jimena grabbed Catty's wrist. "Let's go to a real party."

"Where?" Catty asked, shoving her way around a guy and girl making out.

"Rockout."

"Is it still open?" Catty asked, hoping it was. Rockout was an after-hours club where kids from Turney High hung out. She'd heard about it but had never gone.

"Yeah, but you've got to know someone to know where it reopened," Jimena answered.

"Cool." Catty followed Jimena outside. "Maybe the night's not going to be a total bust."

Jimena's car was parked in front. Neon lights outside Planet Bang flashed across the hood.

Catty buckled herself in as Jimena turned the ignition key. Music blasted from every side, making the dashboard shudder, as the car rolled away.

Twenty minutes later, they rode down a street filled with parked cars. Jimena came to a stop, and they climbed out. Catty looked around the deserted lot. Broken glass sparkled in the moonlight. The smells of dust and brackish water filled the cold air. A breeze eased around them, bringing with it the whooshing sounds of traffic from a nearby freeway.

"Come on." Jimena started walking toward a small, cinder-block building, her heels clicking nicely on the pavement.

Catty followed beside her. They had gone only a little way when an odd vibration shimmied through the ground and traveled up Catty's legs. She looked at Jimena. "It's under us?"

"Los Angeles is filled with storm drains. Some of them are huge; they were set up as air-raid shelters back in the fifties." Jimena opened the door, and hard-hitting rock music rushed up a steep stairwell.

"Ready for some real partying?" Jimena tossed Catty a sly look and started down the steps.

Catty entered behind her and closed the door. Darkness surrounded her. Cautiously, she headed after Jimena, her fingers brushing along the damp, concrete walls.

"Vamp it up," Jimena yelled as they neared the security guards standing in dim light at the bottom of the stairs.

The guard with the short curly black hair smiled as if he recognized Jimena and waved them through without collecting admission.

Catty stepped into a vast, underground room.

Kids danced wildly, swirling glow sticks, making purple, blue, and gold squiggles in the air. Only a few looked cranked up. Then Catty saw Kyle, sandwiched between two girls, and she caught her breath. She turned back, but Jimena had left her and was talking to two guys near a corner roped off with Christmas garlands and glow sticks.

"Want to dance?" someone shouted from behind her.

Catty spun around and stared up at Kyle. She

tilted her head and tried to smile, but seeing him made her too nervous to flirt. What was there about him that caused her to feel so good, yet so uncomfortable?

"You look hot tonight," he said above the music. "You always do."

She licked her thumb, pressed it on her hip and made a hissing sound. She immediately felt stupid for the move and was glad it was too dark for him to see her blush.

The DJ put on another song, and the music thumped through her. Suddenly, she didn't care how embarrassed she felt. She started dancing. Kyle's eyes lingered on her, but instead of feeling upset by his boldness, she was filled with fiery anticipation. She closed her eyes and let herself become lost in the song, enjoying the feel of her body moving so close to his.

The music changed to a faster beat, and everyone sang along. Catty opened her eyes. Kyle brushed back her hair; then his hand slid around her, pulling her deeper into the crowd, glow sticks whirling around them.

She stared at him, loving the way he looked back at her.

Without warning, the music stopped, and kids shoved passed them, heading for the portable toilets.

"You're an incredible dancer," Catty said.

He put his hands on her waist and eased her closer to him. "I love to dance."

"So why do you always hang out in the back at Planet Bang?" Catty asked.

A slow, sultry smile stretched across his face. "Do you watch me there?"

She felt her cheeks turn crimson.

"It's okay. I watch you," he whispered, his breath warm and inviting. "Can I kiss you?"

She swallowed, her throat catching, and couldn't find her voice.

He laughed at her struggle. "I didn't think you'd have such a hard time saying yes after the way you attacked me yesterday."

"I didn't," she started to protest, but his fingers closed her lips.

"I'm teasing." He took her hands and clasped

them around his neck, then drew her tight against him.

Her eyes closed; the wait was unbearable. At last, his lips touched hers; the kiss was sweet and brief.

Abruptly, Kyle pulled away. "I have to leave."

"You want to come over tomorrow after school?" Catty said. "We can order a pizza and watch a movie."

"Maybe." He turned and rushed away.

Her heart sank. Had she done something to upset him? Or was she that bad a kisser? She whirled around and bumped into Jimena, who was staring at her oddly.

"I like Kyle," Catty said defensively. "So what's wrong with that?"

"Nada," Jimena answered. Clearly, something else was on her mind. "Let's go."

They drove back to Catty's house with music blaring, but when they pulled up to the curb, Jimena turned off the ignition, and silence fell around them.

"Are you planning a trip to some exotic

place?" Jimena asked, a perplexed look on her face.

Catty shook her head. "Why?"

"I just got a feeling." Jimena rubbed her stomach as if she had a sudden pain. "Don't go."

"But I'm not planning to go anyplace," Catty said.

Jimena nodded. "You will be, but don't."

A shiver rushed through Catty. What was Jimena seeing this time? She wished she could tell her the truth about what she had once been. "Okay, if something comes up, I won't go."

"Good." Jimena frowned and stared through the windshield as if she were seeing something visible only to her.

"I'll see you tomorrow." Catty climbed from the car.

Jimena waved and drove off, the roar of the car engine fading as she turned the corner.

Catty hurried up to the front porch and pulled the key from under the mat. She unlocked the door as a breeze stirred the wind chimes, and slipped inside. She grabbed a handful of chocolate-chip cookies from the kitchen, then hurried up the stairs to her bedroom.

Moonlight fell across her bed, and in the milky light she saw the Scroll, its gold borders shimmering. A sudden wind brushed branches against her window, and the scratching sound made her turn with a start. At the same moment, she became aware of someone standing in the dark behind her, and the cookies fell from her hand.

CHAPTER FOURTEEN

"KYLE?" CATTY ASKED, her mind rushing for an explanation. "You stole the manuscript?"

He walked toward her, his steps slow and easy. "Last night at the museum, I found it in the stairwell."

"You broke into the museum?" She plopped down on the edge of her bed and brushed her hands through her hair. When Vanessa had dropped the Scroll, Catty had thought one of the guards had picked it up, but now she saw that it could have been Kyle. The light had been dim in the stairwell, and she had been panicked, trying to pull Vanessa away.

"I just walked in," Kyle continued. "Alarms were going off, and it was chaos inside."

"But why would you bring the manuscript to me?" Catty asked. Then she glanced at Kyle, and her heart sank. "You were playing me, weren't you?"

"I wasn't." He sat next to her, his fingers caressing her shoulder. "Why would you think that?"

She jerked her arm away. "You knew I was totally crushing on you, and now you expect me to hide the Scroll for you until you can sell it. I won't. I'm not one of those girls who'll do anything for a guy."

A flirty smile crossed his face. "Are you sure?"

She stood, rage pushing her other emotions aside. "There's no way I'm going to spend the rest of my life in jail because I like some loser."

"Loser?" The smile fell from his face. "Why are you calling me a loser?"

Catty sighed. "I can't believe that's what you're concerned about after you've stolen something this valuable. Aren't you scared of being arrested?"

She grabbed the Scroll and stood still for a moment, cringing at the strange feel of the parchment vibrating beneath her fingers. The tremor raced up her arms. The calligraphy shone with a cold light as if greeting her and urging her to read it. She felt gripped by its beauty and unable to pull her eyes away.

"What's wrong?" Kyle asked, breaking the Scroll's hold on her.

"I'm taking the Scroll back to the museum." Immediately her goddess power stormed through her. Her skin tingled and twitched with energy as a lustrous aura encircled her. She didn't care if Kyle did see her fall into the tunnel. It wasn't as though he were going to remember, and even if he did, so what?

But before the air split open, Kyle grabbed

her wrist. "I know what you are, Catty."

Her energy jammed itself back inside her, and she clenched her teeth against the sudden pain. "What? A fool?"

"You're a Goddess," he whispered. "A Daughter of the Moon."

A dry whistle escaped her lips and her body filled with sudden fear. It ricocheted through her, quickly turning to terror. "You're a Follower?"

"No." He looked sad. "Something much worse."

Catty took her moon amulet in her hands, but it wasn't shining in warning. Still, she took slow, cautious steps away from him, her muscles tensing; she was ready to run.

"I've been sent to take you to your father."

"My father?" Catty felt dazed. The parchment seemed to sense her turmoil and thrummed beneath her fingers with more intensity than before. She set it on her desk.

"He said I'd have to show you the Scroll to convince you that I was telling the truth."

Catty leaned against the wall, considering what Kyle was saying.

"I'll keep you safe," he went on. "I promise."

"I want to meet my father," she whispered hoarsely, her chest filling with an old longing. But her father was also her enemy, a powerful member of the Atrox's Inner Circle. She couldn't trust him, so how could she trust Kyle?

"Let's go, then." Kyle reached for her hand.

Catty hesitated. "Why doesn't he come here?"

"He doesn't like this world," Kyle explained. "I'm supposed to take you to his home in Nefandus."

"Nefandus? I've never heard of that," Catty said and began to tremble. "In Latin, *nefandus* means 'not to be spoken of.'"

Kyle nodded, then spoke in a low, rushed voice. "It's a parallel world created by the Atrox. Members of the Inner Circle and some Followers live there. We don't have much time if we're going to go."

Suddenly Catty felt dizzy and grabbed the edge of her desk. "How do you know about this place if you're not a Follower?"

"I lived there once," Kyle answered quietly.

Catty stared at him, suddenly remembering Jimena's warning. Was this the dangerous journey she had seen in Catty's future?

CHAPTER FIFTEEN

HALF AN HOUR LATER, Kyle and Catty ran down an empty street in Chinatown, the quick clicking of their steps the only sound disturbing the night. They hurried past the dark curio shops and herbal pharmacies displaying snake potions and ginseng. Rich, spicy fragrances still lingered in the air from the closed restaurants.

"Hurry," Kyle said as he stepped through the old Chinatown gateway. "The door between the two worlds only opens when Algol blinks."

"Algol?" Catty followed Kyle past the pagoda-style buildings to a small storefront with the words IT PUN FORTUNE READING written across the window.

"The demon star." Kyle pointed at the clear, black sky. "It's the eye of Medusa, in the constellation of Perseus. When it blinks, we go."

"Where?" Catty studied the plaza between the stores. "Do they beam us up or something?"

"You'll see," Kyle said, still looking up at the sky.

Gradually the brightness of the star dimmed as if the eye were closing.

"How does that happen?" Catty asked, surprised.

Kyle took her hand and walked forward. "Algol is actually two stars revolving around each other. It's called an eclipsing binary."

"Are we going to walk through the window?" Catty followed reluctantly.

"Hurry." Kyle increased his pace.

Catty gasped, certain Kyle was going to shatter the glass of the window.

But, instead, the red-painted storefront

blurred, and a film covered Catty, clinging like a moist membrane. In the same moment, numbness swept through her as if a colossal shot of anesthetic had deadened her body. She froze, unable to move, but before she could panic, a dull throb awakened her senses, and she stumbled forward into an impossibly dense fog.

Sluggish mists rolled around her, the cold prickling over her, snooping and nuzzling as if it were trying to assess what kind of intruder she was.

"I do know this place," she whispered, her teeth chattering. "I was a prisoner here in these vapors once."

Even now, the memory terrified her. She and her friends had been fighting Lambert, a member of the Inner Circle, and when Catty had tried to save Vanessa from his attack, the force of his power had hit Catty instead, sending her into this world of nothingness. It had been a long time before the others had been able to rescue her.

When Kyle didn't answer, Catty whirled around. "Kyle?"

He wasn't there.

Clouds thickened, encircling her. "Where are you?" she cried.

Suddenly, the roar of gushing water surrounded her. Frantic, she thrashed in the milky air, searching for Kyle, and started to rise.

"I should have warned you about the passing." Kyle grabbed her hand, and his touch brought a different world into sharp focus. "It's frightening the first time."

Catty squinted, her feet hit the ground, and she tried to take in everything she saw. She stood on a street lined with tall, narrow houses. Overhead, water spouted from the mouths of gargoyles and splashed noisily onto the sidewalks.

The setting sun peeked through the black clouds on the horizon, and dazzling gold fire streaked across the wet, cobblestoned road.

Kyle looked amused. "It's impossible for outsiders to see in Nefandus. Without a talisman or a resident to guide them, they remain trapped in the vapors."

As if to prove what he was saying, he

wrenched his hand away, and in the same instant the street vanished, replaced by swarming, gray mists.

"It's one last obstacle to protect the Atrox's world," he said, his voice reaching her from the dense fog. "In case an outsider accidentally stumbles through one of the portals."

Then he clasped Catty's hand again, and the towers, turrets, chimneys, and gables came back.

As the sun slid below the horizon, its last rays shot fire over the dwindling clouds. The embers fluttered in the black sky, becoming lurid, red stars.

"Why does the night look so different here?" Catty asked, awestruck.

"It's an artificial sky," Kyle explained. "The Atrox despises the moon and doesn't want to feel its glow."

They walked past a line of trees that stirred with frenetic energy, even though no breeze moved the air. Curious, Catty stepped under the branches, pulling Kyle with her, and gazed up.

Dark forms rippled through the leaves.

Instinct told her that the raven-black shapes slithering around each other were Followers, stuck in their own kind of traffic jam. Powerful Followers could dissolve into shadows and travel that way, like ghosts.

Kyle gently guided her back.

"How does Nefandus exist next to our world?" she asked, staring up at the murky apparitions that still slid sinuously over the treetops.

"Not *next to,*" Kyle said. "This world is superimposed over the one you know."

"How can that be?" Catty stopped in front of a hedge of roses. The blossoms flooded the night with sweet vapor. As she touched a petal, the spindly branches squirmed toward her, and a thorn nicked her arm. She jerked back, surprised, and started walking again.

"Everything is made of atoms," Kyle explained. "But there are spaces between the atoms, and in those spaces are the atoms that create Nefandus."

Catty nodded. "So, the two realms are interlocked?"

"Yes." Kyle started to say something more, but before he could, a disquieting heaviness fell over them, and a flurry of sparks burst into the air.

"Regulators," Kyle whispered, fear in his eyes. "They police the Followers."

"I know what they are." Catty stepped away, grasping Kyle's hand tightly and hoping he didn't notice the way her fingers had begun trembling. "How could they have discovered us so soon?"

Kyle led her into a dark alley. "Maybe they're not looking for us, but just wondering who's walking on the street."

Two Regulators materialized, their long capes settling around their lumpish legs. Coronas of electrostatic bolts buzzed about their misshapen heads.

"When Regulators come into my world," Catty whispered, repelled by their brute ugliness, "they disguise their appearance."

"They don't need to, here." Kyle slipped deeper into the darkness, pulling her with him. "Come on."

They turned and ran down the twisting

passageway, splashing through muddy puddles. Catty sensed eyes peering down at them from the windows in the buildings.

In the next street, which was larger, lanterns swayed from iron brackets set high in a wrought-iron railing decorated with spikes and curlicues. The shimmering lights skipped around Catty and Kyle as they walked up a flagstone path to a large, austere house and crossed the veranda.

Jade dragons stood on either side of the door, and flames shot from their mouths like flicking tongues. The fire was reflected off stained-glass panels depicting devils. With each fluttering of the blaze, the demons seemed to bend and skid across the panes.

Catty felt sick with nervousness. Her expectations were rising, but so was her fear. She breathed through her mouth, trying to quell the nervousness in her stomach.

Kyle caught her look. "Are you feeling sick? The fires burn by magic, but sometimes the fumes make newcomers ill."

She nodded, not bothering to tell him the

real reason she was overcome with dizziness. She had been stupid to come alone. She should have called Vanessa or Serena, but she was always impetuous. Now she wished she were more like Vanessa, serious and thoughtful.

Kyle tapped the silver ring hanging on the door, and the strange creatures imprisoned in the stained glass shifted position to see who was visiting.

The door opened.

"Please, come in." A boy, younger and shorter than Catty, invited them inside, his unblinking black eyes intense against his pallid skin. He turned and walked barefoot over the marble floors, his jeans rolled up to his ankles, the short sleeves of his T-shirt falling below his elbows. He looked as though he'd stolen his clothing from a much larger person.

Catty glanced at Kyle.

"Follow him," Kyle whispered. "He's one of your father's *servi*."

"A slave?" She watched the boy.

He picked up a red cloak from a long bench

and handed it to Catty. Only then did she realize how she must look. Mud splattered her bare legs and skirt, and the designs she had so carefully drawn on her hands and stomach earlier had been smeared into dark blotches. She felt embarrassed that this was the way her father would see her after all these years.

Kyle flashed a smile. "I guess your father has certain rules about modesty."

Catty shot him a look in return and took the cloak. The boy stood on tiptoe to help wrap the silky material around her shoulders. Then he appraised her and, apparently satisfied, led them past a polished oak staircase with heavy balusters.

At the end of the hallway, he opened double doors. Brass hinges creaked, and Catty and Kyle entered an overly warm room.

A man with thinning dark hair stood in front of the fireplace, close to the whipping flames. Soot blackened the white marble, changing from one spectral form to another before vanishing into smoke.

"Father?" Catty asked, not sure how she felt.

Her pulse jittered, her heart unable to find the right rhythm.

The man turned slowly, his eyes gentle rather than menacing. She had never imagined that her father would look so pleasant.

"Catty." He called her name, his voice at once familiar and strange.

Before she was even aware of it, he seeped inside her mind and released his memories of her childhood. His love burst into her awareness with a suddenness that made her stagger.

Without thinking, she dropped Kyle's hand and ran to her father. The world turned back to buckling mists, but she ignored the fog and continued running. She lunged forward, and when she fell against her father, the room came back, and her lungs filled with the acrid smells from the fireplace.

She breathed deeply, trying to catch the scent of her father, her mind filled with vague memories of licorice and days spent outside. Or had he put that recollection into her mind?

He held her tightly, his heartbeat thudding

in her ear, then pulled back and gazed down at her. She hadn't realized how tall he was until that moment. She came up only to his shoulder.

He smiled. "I love you so much, Catty."

"Why did you want to see me?" she asked, holding her breath and hoping his answer would be the one she needed to hear. She had memories of her own stashed away, of days spent lying on her bed, thinking about her father and wondering where he was. Did he miss her and want to build a relationship with her before she turned seventeen? She desperately wanted him in her life, and she didn't care that they were enemies, sworn to destroy each other. More than anything, she needed to be able to trust him.

His smile fell away. His pale blue eyes looked pained. He was obviously searching for the right words.

Catty's shoulders slumped forward. It wasn't going to be the answer she wanted.

But before he could speak, a chill rushed up her spine, and she sensed another presence in the room. Without warning, the fire exploded. Red embers and wisps of smoke pulsated around her.

The air thrummed, and a Regulator formed from the falling cinders. Its contact with the Atrox's evil had warped its skull and distorted its spine. As it stared at her, a grotesque imitation of a smile crossed its rotting face.

She knew she shouldn't hesitate, but she paused for the briefest moment, unwilling to believe her father could betray her, and then fear broke her inertia, and she jerked away from her father.

But before she could escape into the unfurling vapors, the Regulator grabbed her and pulled her against his soft, warm flesh. His steamy breath condensed on her lips, the stench filling her lungs.

"It was all a trap!" she cried, angry tears blinding her.

She tried to use her power to open the tunnel and escape, but her energy didn't build. She clutched her amulet, hoping it would give her strength. The charm felt like an ordinary stone against her palm.

"Your goddess powers don't work in Nefandus," her father said matter-of-factly.

She caught a look in his eyes. Was he trying to tell her something more?

Then she glanced at Kyle. He had said he wasn't a Follower, but something worse. If she hadn't been so anxious to meet her father she would have questioned him. She had let herself be deceived too easily.

The Regulator started to dissolve. In seconds, he would take her to the Atrox. She needed to break free, but even if she did, how could she escape Nefandus?

CHAPTER SIXTEEN

"GO!" KYLE SHOUTED, his eyes darting around as he looked for a way out.

"How?" Catty screamed back, her hands becoming fuzzy as her molecules stretched out, melding with those of the Regulator. Her mouth filled with his rancid odor, the taste gagging her. She was powerless against his pull, and her cells continued to loosen.

She elbowed the Regulator's stomach, but her arm only sank into his warm, wet flesh. She winced and pulled back, a scream building in her lungs. Before it could burst into the air, she closed her eyes and pictured the moon. Her lips formed the prayer that had always helped her in the past. *"O Mater Luna, Regina nocis, adiuvo me nunc."*

Hope surged through her, and she broke free, but without the Regulator touching her, the room dissolved into the surreal landscape of gray clouds.

The Regulator shrieked in defeat and anger, his churlish scream striking Catty like a shock wave.

Catty sprinted blindly forward with nothing to guide her and tripped, twisting her ankle. Pain shot up her leg. Then a small hand clamped on to her wrist and the dark hallway came into sudden focus. She stared into the unblinking eyes of her father's young slave.

He tossed her an impish grin, and, still holding on to her, began running down a paneled corridor, his bare feet slapping against the marble floor. Abruptly he stopped and leaned against a portion of the wall, his heel kicking at the baseboard molding.

The panel swung open and the boy led her into a secret passageway. The wall closed against her back, nudging her forward and plunging her into complete darkness. A sputtering sound surrounded her, and then spiraling flames ignited in wall brackets.

"Come." The boy led her down steep, creaking stairs, his tiny fingers digging into her skin.

"Do you know how to get out of Nefandus?" she asked.

He nodded, and, at the bottom of the steps, he opened a door that led to the street.

Catty stepped out onto the cobblestoned pavement, relief flooding through her. She turned, waiting for the boy to join her outside, but he jerked his hand back and slammed the door.

Immediately the sharp clarity of the Nefandus night dissolved into veils of fog. Mists whispered around her, caressing her face.

"Let me back in!" She lurched forward, trying to find the door. But what had been there only moments before, solid and palpable, was now gone.

Muffled footsteps and voices surrounded her. She cried out and sprinted into the dreamscape, pain flaring in her leg.

At last she stopped, too disoriented to continue, and, in the absence of even her own footsteps, she was left in complete silence. The utter stillness frightened her. The haze became thicker, obscuring all visibility and sweeping a terrible coldness around her. She closed her eyes, trying to sense where she had entered Nefandus, but she remembered nothing that could help her now.

Catty continued walking until her legs ached and blisters formed on her toes and heels. She was certain she had been climbing steadily upward for the last few minutes, and now she was afraid to go farther, for fear of plummeting over the edge of a cliff.

The temperature continued to drop as blue ice crystals formed in the clouds and gathered on her skin and in her hair.

She sensed something watching her and tensed, turning slowly, hating the helpless feeling that overwhelmed her now. Maybe Regulators had found her and were lurking in the mists, watching with amusement as she panicked.

She moved her hand slowly through the haze, trying to see anything that might guide her, but the air only rippled, ice flakes floating around her like diamond dust, and then she knew with sudden clarity that she would never find her way back to her own world.

Tears froze on her cheeks. The air leached life from her. She was going to die alone, far from her friends and her mother. She thought of Kendra now, remembering something Kendra had told her after her pet canary had died, years ago.

"*We're only spirits, visiting earth in our bodies,*" Catty whispered as she sat down on the cold ground. She wrapped the red cloak tightly around her and tried to accept her own death. "*Our spirits live on.*"

CHAPTER SEVENTEEN

A HAND COVERED Catty's lips, locking a startled scream inside her throat. The unexpected touch brought Nefandus back in striking detail, and the sweet, pungent fumes from the magic fires curled into her lungs.

"Don't move." Kyle whispered against her temple. "It's me."

She nodded, then glanced down, shocked, seeing pinnacles and spires below her. She was sitting high above the houses, balanced precariously on the outer edge of a flight of iron stairs that led to a bell tower, her bare legs dangling in the cold air. She tried to swing onto the steps, but her feet felt like dead weights.

"Careful," Kyle warned, and he grasped her arm, pulling her up.

At last she stood and took a faltering step. Her knees buckled and she wrenched back, teetering over the edge, the rooftops whirling below her.

Kyle gathered her against him, his warmth seeping into her, reviving her. "I've been looking for you."

"Like I wasn't trying to find you," Catty snapped, through chattering teeth, as she gratefully pressed her face against his chest.

"Can you walk?" He started guiding her down, his feet clanging against the metal.

"I think I can." She struggled to take a step.

"Try," he said. "We only have minutes before the demon star blinks again."

Catty sensed his urgency, and her heartbeat

quickened. She didn't want to be trapped in Nefandus a moment longer. She shuffled forward, the stairs rattling and swaying beneath her numb feet. "Have three days passed already?"

"Time is different here," Kyle explained, his eyes filling with new concern. "Do you want me to carry you?"

"No." She shook her head and forced her legs to move more quickly. "I can do it."

When they finally reached the street below, Kyle glanced at his watch. It was different from any Catty had seen before. The face looked like a map of the stars.

Kyle caught her curious expression. "I use it to follow the earth's sky when I'm inside Nefandus," he explained, pressing her forward. "We have to hurry."

Catty hesitated. Kyle was her only hope, but could she trust him?

"What now?" Kyle didn't bother to hide his impatience.

Her fear was immense. She was afraid he would let go of her if she angered him now, but she had to say what was on her mind. "How can I trust you after what happened?"

"That wasn't my fault." His jaw clenched.

"But—"

"I'm leaving," he interrupted, and started forward, loosening his grip on her hand. "And if you want to live, you'll come with me."

"All right." She took a long breath of air, resolute, and followed him, running from archway to porch stoop, hiding in the black shadows near the houses.

She tried to stop the negative thoughts that were buzzing in her head, but she couldn't quiet the nagging sensation that Kyle was dragging her to another encounter with Regulators.

At last, they turned down a familiar street lined with tall, narrow houses, and she was instantly overwhelmed by the sweet fragrance of roses. Gargoyles sat on rooftops, their grotesque heads projecting from rain gutters. Catty recognized the neighborhood, and hope surged through her. She wanted nothing more than to be home, taking a long bubble bath and drinking a cup of frothy hot chocolate.

They neared the cramped passage between two brick houses where they had entered Nefandus and started walking more quickly, anxious to leave, but a sudden change in the air made them stop.

"They've found our entrance," Kyle whispered, edging back.

Blue sparks rippled across the darkness, spinning somber shadows into a thickening blackness. Then a Regulator materialized in the whirling shadows and stepped toward them, the air trembling with his power. Wiry hairs jutted from his ears and nose, and seeping sores sealed his eyes closed, but even stone-blind he seemed to sense them and lumbered forward with deadly intent.

The Regulator's noxious odor filled Catty's lungs, and she jerked back, coughing.

"What are we going to do now?" Catty squeezed against Kyle, holding her free hand over her mouth and nose.

"There are other exits," Kyle said, stepping backward and pulling her with him. "But most of them are more dangerous."

"It can't be worse than trying to outrun this guy," Catty said.

Unexpectedly the Regulator shrieked, making a terrifyingly brutal sound. The scream echoed off the walls with a force that made Catty cringe.

"He's calling others." Kyle scowled.

More shadows began to pull together, writhing into phantom forms that stretched and twisted into Regulators.

"We can't fight so many." Catty pulled Kyle's arm, trying to make him move. "What are we waiting for?"

"They're slower when they're visible," Kyle explained.

Catty glanced at the creatures' misshapen feet and understood.

"Now!" Kyle screamed as the last Regulator formed and shambled toward them.

Catty jolted back, then turned and sprinted, her legs pumping hard in spite of the pain shooting through her.

The ground rumbled with the heavy footsteps of the Regulators.

Catty strained, trying to keep up with Kyle. She glanced back, and her heart skipped a beat as the first Regulator dissolved, his spectral shadow spiraling into a cloud and speeding after them.

"What are we going to do?" Catty screamed, her footsteps slowing in surrender.

CHAPTER EIGHTEEN

"COME ON!" KYLE yelled back, yanking on her arm.

Catty quickened her pace and followed Kyle up a zigzagging road to the top of a hill. A breeze flew around them, scattering leaves and bringing the haunting music of a cello from a house perched on an outcropping of jagged rocks. Kyle ran through a maze of twisting tree trunks, then across a grassy field, pulling Catty with him toward the edge of a cliff.

She stared down at the brightly lit streets below.

"Jump!" Kyle yelled, preparing to leap forward.

"Are you crazy?" Catty held back, grabbing Kyle's wrist with her free hand and stopping him. She didn't have the willpower to make herself dive over the ledge.

"Have faith." Kyle looked at her encouragingly.

Catty turned. Shadows shifted beneath the long line of trees, and the Regulators became visible.

She sucked in air and nodded. "Okay."

"Screaming helps." Kyle held her hand more tightly, his tension obvious.

"Like you needed to tell me that," Catty shouted.

She sprang forward and threw herself off the steep face of the hill. She plunged through the air, legs kicking. The wind whistled around her, shrieking in her ears, her own yells joining the wind's song. She tumbled downward, fingernails digging into Kyle's skin, her stomach churning violently.

Suddenly a thin membrane congealed around her, stopping her fall and freezing her in the boundary between the two worlds. Her body felt deadened, all sensation lost to her, and then, as before, a dull ache pulsed through her, awakening her senses, and she stumbled forward, stretching through the moist film and into the soothing night air. Palm fronds clicked lazily overhead.

Catty stood still, disoriented, her back stiff against a brick wall, and then the rich, spicy smells of fried dumplings and barbecue swept into her lungs, and her stomach cramped with hunger. Her eyes snapped open.

She was back in Los Angeles, gazing into Kyle's beautiful blue eyes, the upswept eaves and undulating gables of Chinatown glistening in a bright array of flashing neon lights behind him. Traffic sounds and thundering music added to the clamor of people rushing down the sidewalk, pushing past them.

"It's Friday night," Kyle said, easing her away

from the dark recess in the building. "I don't think anyone saw us step from the wall. It's too dark in there."

Catty glanced quickly around. Everyone looked too busy and lost in their own thoughts to have noticed their sudden appearance. She sighed in relief.

"Thank you." She hugged Kyle, then pulled away, laughing, and twirled into the crowd. She lifted her face to the moon in gratitude, her body soaking in its luxurious light. Her cloak spiraled about her like a bright, shiny flame.

At last she stopped, breathless, and bumped into an elderly couple carrying groceries. The white-haired woman bustled around Catty disapprovingly.

Quickly, Catty glanced down at her mud-stained legs. Her toes were blistered and bleeding, her sandals caked with dirt and grass. A sudden draft made her touch her chest. Her top had been torn from her shoulder and was flapping loose, exposing too much. She yanked the cloak around her, heat rising to her cheeks, and glanced at Kyle, hoping he hadn't noticed. She stepped back into the dark alcove.

"Sorry." He shrugged. "I was going to tell you."

"When?" Catty asked. "Next year?"

Kyle touched her cheek, his eyes suddenly serious. "Maybe."

She caught her breath. His caress surprised her, and she felt suddenly shy. His hand slid down her neck to her shoulder, his fingers working the silky cloak until his palm was against her skin again, sliding down her arm. She eased forward, her lips parting.

"Let's go to my loft," he whispered, his breath mingling with hers.

CHAPTER NINETEEN

BEFORE CATTY COULD answer, a thought came to her.

"Will the Regulators follow us out?" Catty asked.

"Probably not, or they would have come here already." Kyle gathered her into his arms, ignoring the people bumping around them. "I'm sorry, Catty. I never meant to put you in so much danger. Your father swore it would be safe for me to take you to his home."

"You can't trust his kind," Catty answered, her voice finding its natural tone again. "Who are you? Why did you live there?"

Kyle took her hand and started walking. "I was a *servus,* a slave."

"Like the little boy in my father's house?" Catty adjusted the cloak, pulling it over her shoulders and pinching it shut, her bare feet cold on the sidewalk. "Did Regulators kidnap you?"

He shook his head. "I went there to rescue a friend."

"What happened to him?" Catty asked.

"At first I'd thought he had run away from home," Kyle explained. "Later, I found out he'd been lured into Nefandus with promises of learning magic."

"Who got him to go there?" Catty shuddered, remembering the cold mists.

"I don't know." Kyle shrugged. "I tried to rescue him, but instead I was captured and enslaved myself."

Catty felt terrible for the bad things she had thought about Kyle in the past. His loner behavior and bad attitude made sense to her now. "How did you escape?"

"A monk helped me." Kyle stopped in front of a food cart.

"A monk?" Steam wreathed around Catty, filling the air with the savory aroma of soy sauce, cabbage, and pork.

"The monk showed me the portals, then told me about a black diamond that fell from the crown of the Atrox centuries back." Kyle bought two steamed meat buns and handed one to Catty. "If I can find it, then I will be free, and you and I won't have to worry about Regulators taking us back."

They started walking again, threading through the crowd.

"I've never heard of a black diamond." Catty thought of Maggie, wondering why she hadn't told them about something that important. Sorrow flooded through her; she missed Maggie desperately.

"Your father offered to tell me the location of the jewel if I brought you to him." Kyle turned and looked at her, his voice beginning to sound drowsy. "He told me how much he wanted to see you. I didn't know he had another plan."

"I believe you," she answered, lost in his gaze.

He cradled her face in his hands with a sweet look of longing. Her hands slipped around his waist, her body relishing his closeness.

"Let's go to your place," she murmured, surprising herself, and at the same time praying he hadn't forgotten his invitation.

He searched her face. "I was afraid you'd be unforgiving," he whispered. "For everything that had happened."

"My father betrayed me, not you," she said, her voice barely audible. She didn't want to waste the moment with words. "Kiss me."

She closed her eyes, and then his lips were on hers, soft and hesitating, making her yearn for more.

Without warning, someone grabbed Catty's arm and swung her around.

CHAPTER TWENTY

"WHERE HAVE YOU been?" Jimena held a stack of yellow papers, the edges ruffling in the breeze. "I've been plastering flyers with your picture all over L.A."

Catty took one, and a chill passed through her as she stared down at the blurry photograph of her own face, the word MISSING boldly printed on the page. She wondered if Vanessa, Serena, and Tianna had tried to stop Jimena and failed.

Only a few weeks back, Catty's absence wouldn't have alarmed Jimena; she would have assumed Catty was time-traveling. Now, the care and concern in her eyes made Catty want to cry. "I'm sorry. I know it looks—"

"You're right, it *looks.*" Jimena glowered. "You can't imagine what I thought had happened to you."

Sudden apprehension curled through Catty's stomach. Maybe Jimena had had another premonition.

"I'm going to take you home." Jimena grabbed Catty's arm and glared at Kyle, daring him to contradict her.

Kyle backed away, the wind tousling his hair. "I'll call you, Catty." He waved, then turned and sprinted into the crowd.

"Come on." Jimena started toward the public parking lot.

Catty could feel the anxiety building inside Jimena. She was sure Jimena wanted to say more. "Are you all right?" she asked.

"Why shouldn't I be?"

A sudden gust whistled around them, snatching the flyers from Jimena's hand. The yellow papers twisted into the air, stringing out like a kite's tail. Then the wind stopped, and the sheets fell to the ground, fluttering uneasily around them.

Jimena kicked some of the papers aside, and finally snapped, "You're going to get a bad reputation if you hang out with *tipos* like Kyle and do what you did."

Her accusation shot through Catty. "You think I was . . . that I . . ."

"I think you let him own you," Jimena answered.

Catty stopped dead and stared at Jimena in disbelief. "That's not what happened."

"Then what did happen?" Jimena folded her arms over her chest, her gold rings catching the street light.

Catty hesitated, wishing she could tell Jimena everything. "You know me better than that," she said finally.

"I thought I did." Jimena looked suddenly

weary, her eyes searching, as if she were waiting for Catty to say more.

"You're just going to have to believe me." Catty didn't want to lie, but she couldn't tell Jimena the truth, either.

Jimena nodded, then started walking, her steps slower now, as if she were thinking.

By the time they reached the car, the wind raced around them, slapping their hair and clothes about their bodies. Jimena paused at the car door, a haunted expression on her face, as if she were seeing something visible only to her.

"What?" Catty asked, a grim feeling building inside her. She was certain Jimena was having a premonition, and she had never known Jimena to be forewarned about anything good.

Jimena shook her head, and the wind grabbed her scarf, twirling it out behind her. "I'm just having weird thoughts lately."

"Can you tell me?" Catty shouted over the screeching blasts of wind. She slid into the passenger seat and slammed the door.

Jimena took her place behind the steering

wheel. She turned the ignition key, but instead of backing out of the parking slot, she sat and stared at the trash spinning up the side of a gray building. Shoppers rushed down the sidewalk, heads bent into the wind.

"I'm scared, Catty," she whispered as a sudden gust jostled the car.

"About what?" Catty touched Jimena's cold fingers, trying to comfort her. She had a nagging feeling that Jimena was on the verge of a breakdown, and it made her feel helpless and hollow inside.

"It's just that . . ." Jimena pressed her foot on the accelerator and backed up, then shifted into drive and eased out of the parking lot. "I'm remembering things I couldn't know."

"Maybe it's something you read about and—"

"It's not like that," Jimena interrupted. "I'm not talking about something I studied in school. I'm talking about memories. *¿Me entiendes?*"

"I'm sure there's an explanation," Catty said, with a confidence she didn't feel.

"Ojala." Jimena nodded but didn't say more.

By the time they reached Catty's house, the winds had cleared the sky and blown down branches and leaves. Palm fronds lay scattered across the front lawn.

"You want to come in?" Catty asked, wondering if it were safe to leave Jimena alone.

"My *abuelita* is expecting me," Jimena answered softly.

Catty nodded and climbed from the car, then leaned back in through the window. "Thanks for putting up all those posters."

Jimena turned, her black eyes glistening. "Catty . . ."

"Yeah?" Catty's heart pounded in anticipation.

"You've got to make some decisions soon." Jimena looked as if she were forcing herself to say something that confused her.

"About what?" Catty asked, not sure she wanted to hear the answer.

"I just know you need to trust your heart." Jimena shrugged and waved. "*Chaucito.*"

Catty watched the car pull away from the

curb, then rushed to the porch, anxious to get inside. The frantic music of wind chimes jingled overhead. She lifted the mat, snatched up the key, unlocked the door, and slid into the dark living room.

Wind skated over the roof, its wail echoing through the empty house. She dropped the key on the glass coffee table and ran upstairs to the bathroom. She took a long shower, letting the hot spray work out the cold and pain in her back and legs, and then, after she had washed her hair, she turned off the water, wrapped a towel around her, and hurried to her bedroom.

The Scroll still lay on the middle of her desk, where she had left it.

Catty started to reach for a comb, when something about the Scroll caught her eye. She stood, frozen. Wind sighed around the house, brushing tree branches against the window screens and sweeping shadows across her desk, but she was certain that what she had seen had not been a trick of the light. She switched on her desk lamp and swallowed, her mouth dry, and then she leaned closer, studying the Scroll's borders.

Letters were intertwined in the design, as if someone had camouflaged the words. She opened her drawer and pulled out a paper and pencil, then puzzled over the design, jotting down each letter until she had made a sentence.

When she had finished, she read the words out loud: *"Cum oculus daemonis coniveat, ini in terram vetitam."* Then she whispered the translation, "When the demon eye blinks, enter the forbidden land."

A sense of power overwhelmed her. She felt certain that this was the first step. The writing in the body of the manuscript had been only a distraction, in case the Scroll fell into the wrong hands.

She knew the "forbidden land" must be Nefandus, the realm "not to be spoken of." Her heart raced, she knew she had to return there to follow the path.

With new excitement, she nudged the Scroll with her pencil, turning it, searching. She was careful not to touch the parchment, remembering how it had cast a spell on her before. Her intuition told her it was even more dangerous now that she had uncovered its secret. She stared at the intricate patterns, inspecting the small animals and insects hidden within the vines, each miniature now a mystery to unravel. The rich jewel colors flashed with unusual brightness, as if the Scroll were trying to pull her attention away from the delicate drawings in front of her.

For the next three days she slept only when she could no longer keep her eyes open. She let her machine pick up her calls. By Sunday, she had found the third and fourth steps, concealed within the flowing wings of a choir of angels.

The night went by, and Monday morning came. The doorbell rang twice, but she ignored it, certain it was Vanessa pestering her about school. She was too close to completion to stop now. She studied the decorative tendrils and spiky ivy until her vision blurred.

Finally, she had uncovered nine steps. Exhausted, she fell across her bed, but as she drifted into slumber, an eerie humming made her glance up. Leaves scraped against her window. She assumed that their motion across the glass had made the shrill sound. She didn't see the glow coming from the manuscript.

The temperature dropped, and the air filled with hostile forces as the Scroll struggled to untangle its delicate decorations and obliterate the tenth step before Catty found it hidden within the drawing of a tree. The painted borders wiggled, the interwoven designs squirming into the blank margins, trying to unfurl and free the words entwined in the twisting branches.

Catty rolled over, pulling the covers around her, unaware of the danger.

CHAPTER TWENTY-ONE

LATER THAT NIGHT, Catty awakened with a start. The wind pounded against her bedroom window, and at first she thought a strong gust had startled her in her sleep, but then she smelled freshly brewed coffee. She swung her legs over the side of the bed, surprised by the sharp chill in the room.

"Mom?" she called.

When no one answered, she darted into the

dark hallway, certain her mother had come home early. More than anything, she needed to talk to Kendra and tell her everything that had happened. Maybe Kendra would even know something about Nefandus after all her years of translating old Latin manuscripts.

But at the top of the steps, Catty stopped abruptly; she clutched the newel post, and stared down at the living room below. She didn't see anything to explain the alarm rushing through her, but instinct told her something was wrong.

She breathed deeply, trying to settle her nerves. The aroma of coffee filled her lungs again, but this time it held new meaning. Even if her mother had come home unexpectedly, she wouldn't have been drinking coffee at this hour. She'd have been sipping orange-spice herbal tea. Besides, Kendra always awakened her when she returned from a trip. So, who was in the house?

Tree branches lashed back and forth in front of the streetlights outside the downstairs windows, sweeping shadows across the living room. Catty eased her way down the stairs, her arms and legs shaking violently, eyes watchful and expecting Regulators to emerge from the whirling dark.

When she reached the landing, a sudden gust rattled the front door, jiggling locks and dead bolts. She breathed in sharply and, after a pause, crept toward the kitchen. She pressed against the door and peeked in.

Kyle sat at the kitchen table, drinking coffee and thumbing through one of her mother's Latin texts.

"Kyle!" Anger shot through her, replacing her fear. She threw the door open and let it bang against the wall. Glasses rattled in the cupboards.

Kyle flinched, spilling his coffee, then looked up. A slow smile crossed his face. "I didn't mean to wake you yet."

"You scared me to death." Catty stomped into the kitchen and folded her arms over her chest. "What are you doing here?"

"You didn't answer your phone or the door." He grabbed a paper napkin and wiped up the puddle of coffee.

"So you just broke in?"

"I needed to talk to you." He shrugged, as if breaking into a girl's house were perfectly normal. "What was I supposed to do?"

"You're supposed to wait, like everyone else." She surveyed the kitchen. The chain lock hung motionless from the door, her mom's crystal collection sat undisturbed on the windowsill, and the security bar was still in place, locking the glass sliding door to the patio. "How did you get in here?"

He hesitated, an odd twitch in the corner of his eye. "I guess you could say I floated."

"You're a shape-shifter." She slumped into a chair next to the table. "One of them."

"I couldn't let you know everything about me, Catty," he said apologetically. "If I had, you never would have trusted me to take you to Nefandus. I know how much you hate Stanton—"

"You're a Follower?"

"I'm not a Follower, but if I had shown you all my powers from the beginning, I wouldn't have been able to convince you otherwise."

"I wish you had told me the truth." She searched his face, knowing he had used her. How could she have allowed herself to be deceived so easily? She looked down, not wanting him to see her tears.

"I didn't use you, Catty," he said softly.

Her head snapped up. "I didn't say that. I only thought it. Are you able to read my mind, too?"

He grinned sheepishly. "Not as well as Serena can, but I'm better at catching emotions. It's necessary for survival in Nefandus."

Catty raked her fingers through her hair, trying to recall all her steamy daydreams. How many of her sex-hungry thoughts had he caught?

"That time hiding between the bookcases . . ." she began timidly.

"I got those feelings, loud and clear." His smile broadened. "You wanted me to kiss you, but then you switched time—"

"You can't know I traveled into the past!" She stood abruptly, knocking her chair over. "No one knows when I change time."

"I do," he said simply. "When you live in Nefandus, you develop perceptions that people don't have here."

She groaned and rubbed her temples. No wonder it had been so easy for him to use her. He had known from the beginning how infatuated she was.

"What's wrong?" he asked.

"Wrong? I thought you were good at picking up emotions. I feel like a complete fool. Just leave."

"I can't." He stood and stepped toward her.

"Yes, you can." She walked to the back door and started to unlatch the chain lock.

"You need to go back to Nefandus with me, Catty." He took hold of her hand, his fingers clasping hers.

"I'll never go there again," she whispered and leaned her forehead against the doorjamb, but there was no conviction behind her words.

"You have the Scroll," he said, touching her elbow. "But the Keeper is missing, and you need him. I can help you find him."

She jerked back, staring at him, her suspicion rising. "Do you know what happened to Chris?"

"I don't," he said. "But the monk who helped me escape does."

"What did he say?" Catty asked.

"He won't tell me," Kyle replied. "He'll only speak to you. I'm supposed to take you to him."

"Back to Nefandus." Catty eyed Kyle skeptically. She wanted to trust him, but could she?

He held his hand up as though he were taking an oath. "I swear I'm telling the truth."

She studied him. Physically, she was attracted to him, and if she hadn't been a Daughter she could have fallen for him in the biggest way, but she couldn't allow the feelings stirring inside her to get in the way of making the right decision.

"Tell the monk to come here," she said at last.

"He can't," Kyle answered, stroking her bare arm with his finger. "We have to go to him."

Catty shook her head, but her heart was already racing, anticipating the journey. She needed to meet the monk if she were going to find Chris, but why would a man who had withdrawn from life to devote himself to prayer and solitude live in Nefandus? Only Followers lived there.

"He helps the *servi*, Catty," Kyle answered her thoughts, his hand working its way around to her back, caressing her gently.

She stared at him, wondering if she could depend on him. If she went back to Nefandus she'd have to trust him to hold on to her, or she'd be lost in that frightening, foggy world.

"I'm not using you," he said abruptly, as if he understood her conflicting emotions better than she did herself. "My feelings for you are real."

"I want to believe you," she whispered.

His hand slid around her waist, and he pulled her to him, but instead of resisting, she slid her hands over his sweatshirt and chest, enjoying the warmth of his body and the sweet ache rushing through her own. Her breath caught as a thought filled her mind: they were alone; her bed was empty upstairs.

"You have to trust your heart," Kyle whispered, nuzzling her ear.

At first Catty thought he was asking her to take him upstairs; then she realized he was talking about Nefandus, giving her the same advice Jimena had offered her. She tried to silence her mind, but her thoughts kept coming back to her mistrust; she felt certain Kyle was using her even though she didn't understand what he had to gain by it. Still, if there were any chance he was telling the truth, then she had to go with him to help Chris.

"What do you know about the Keeper?" Catty asked finally, her lips moving against his, wondering why he didn't kiss her.

"I know enough about Chris to know he didn't tell you the truth," Kyle answered bluntly.

CHAPTER TWENTY-TWO

CATTY RAN INTO HER room, the scent of Kyle's spicy aftershave still clinging to her hair and cheeks. She tore off her T-shirt, grabbed a black sweater, and pulled it over her head. She tried to figure out what lie Chris might have told her, but her mind kept returning to Kyle. He was the one she couldn't trust. Then she remembered Jimena's advice and took a deep breath, hoping to still her thoughts and hear her heart. But before she could clear her mind, she noticed something on the Scroll.

She stepped closer to her desk, an eerie feeling rushing through her. The borders had altered. The tree on the bottom left side of the manuscript looked oddly bare, as if leaves had fallen from its branches during the night.

"Catty, you have to hurry," Kyle called from downstairs.

"I'm dressing!" she yelled back and pulled on her cropped jeans. She slipped into her sneakers, still studying the florid design. The artwork couldn't have just changed, yet she felt certain the intertwining branches had straightened out.

"We have to go, now!" Kyle shouted, his footsteps pounding up the stairs.

"I'm coming!" She ran into the hallway and slammed into Kyle.

He steadied her, his hands strong and comforting. "We don't have much time."

"Then why don't you just turn us into shadow and take us there?" she snapped. "I thought that's what shape-shifters did."

"And run into Regulators or Followers?" He looked down at her, his breath sweet and warm. "I care about you, Catty, and I don't want you to have to face them again."

For a moment she thought he was going to kiss her. She brazenly hooked her fingers into the front pockets of his jeans, her heart racing with anticipation.

"Don't you ever think of anything else?" he asked.

She opened her eyes.

Irritation flashed across his face, but in the light cast by the lamp in her room she also caught something else before he pulled away. His eyes looked pained. She stared at him, puzzled. "What's wrong?"

"There's no time now." He took her hand, guiding her forward.

"No time?" she asked, descending the stairs behind him. "I thought guys always had time for that."

They ran out into the cold night. A gust howled around them, tousling their hair.

Whatever answer Kyle gave her was whipped away.

"What did you say?" she asked over the wind.

If he heard her question, he didn't respond. He opened the car door and helped her in, then ran around the front and jumped into the driver's seat. He turned the key and gunned the engine. The car pulled away from the curb and blasted down the street.

They rode in silence, her body too aware of his closeness. Kyle pressed the accelerator hard and wrenched the steering wheel, making a sharp left turn into Chinatown. Tires squealed, and the car fishtailed.

He drove two more blocks, then parked, turned off the ignition, opened his door, and glanced at the sky. "We can still make it if we run fast enough."

Catty climbed out and started running after him, her feet hammering on the sidewalk. The demon star looked as if its eye were starting to open. "We're never going to make it!" she yelled, wondering what would happen if she became trapped in the boundary when the portal closed.

"We will," he answered with confidence.

"Dive!" Kyle shouted, and he plunged headfirst toward the storefront of It Pun Fortune Reading.

Catty dove after him, praying that her aim was accurate. The tips of her fingers hit the glass, and she screamed, certain she was going to crash through the window. But the building gave way, and she found herself suspended. A membrane sheathed her. Her body went numb, frozen in midair, and then a blunt pulsing awakened her senses. She fell, tumbling into the roiling vapors. She swiped her hands through empty air, searching for Kyle. "Where are you?" she shouted, her voice echoing oddly.

Immediately clouds gathered around her, the cold mists pawing at her face, seeming to scrutinize her.

Just as she started to panic, Kyle grabbed her wrist, and his touch made Nefandus appear.

A golden haze hung over the city, and

colored its gargoyles, turrets, and rooftops with an amber dust. The sun set, hurling red flames into the black sky. Lanterns hanging from an iron fence sparked, their fires flaring behind the glass in a dazzling fanfare of rainbow lights.

Catty stood in the same narrow street as before. "I thought Regulators had closed this entrance."

"They can't guard all the gates." Kyle started walking. "And they wouldn't think we'd be stupid enough to use the same entrance again."

She stared after him in disbelief. "Is that meant to comfort me? It didn't."

"Come on." He guided her in a different direction, away from the road they had taken the last time.

Instead they circled the remains of an old castle. When they reached the other side, strange music filled the air. The sound vibrated through Catty, filling her with an odd nostalgia; but how could she miss something she had never known?

Kyle stopped beneath a twisted pine tree, his eyes searching and more alert. The spiky needles brushed over them, tickling the back of Catty's neck.

"Be more careful now," he ordered, studying the cobbled street in front of them.

"Right," she answered. "Like I've been reckless up till now."

He threw her a look, then crept stealthily forward, dodging from one shadow to the next, as the music became louder. Abruptly, he stopped and drew Catty toward him.

A couple walked past them, dressed in black velvet and speaking in muffled tones, their hair long and dangling in their eyes.

"Now," Kyle whispered.

Catty dodged across the street and followed Kyle down a narrow path. They ducked under low-hanging branches and circled an outdoor club, the drumbeat booming through her.

She leaned on a tree trunk, her chest on fire, her lungs unable to draw in air. "I have to rest," she whispered.

Through the leaves she watched Followers dressed in black leather and lace dance across the patio. Small fires hanging magically in the air cast flickering lights over their faces.

A guy looked up, his eyes flashing as if he had sensed her presence. He stepped away from the others and bolted over the shrubbery, bearing down on her with a speed that shocked her.

Terror shot through her. "Is he flying?"

Kyle pushed her behind a line of flowering bushes; her chin hit the dirt, and then Kyle fell beside her, his body tight against hers. "Don't move," he whispered.

Adrenaline rushed through Catty. Her muscles ached with the need to run, and her mouth went dry with fear.

The Follower paused, hovering in the air over them, then settled, his feet just skimming the ground, eyes gazing into the darkness. Catty held her breath, fearful he would glance down and see her. His hand grazed the bush, scattering flowers. White petals floated lazily to the ground, covering her face.

The music changed to a slow, sultry song, and glittering dust twirled around the guy. A girl appeared from the gold specks, caressing his arms. A crocheted sweater covered her like a spiderweb, revealing patches of pale skin beneath the mesh.

"It's party time," she said in a petulant voice, her hips swaying against his leg. "What are you doing out here?"

He wrapped an arm around her. "I saw something."

"A night owl?" She laughed in a sly, flirty way, then turned his face toward her, with the tip of her finger. "How can you be searching for *something* when you have me?"

He smiled at her, and then together they dissolved into billowing smoke and twirled back to the dance floor, forming again beneath a glinting flame, already moving in time to the beat.

"Are you all right?" Kyle helped Catty stand and then pulled her behind another tree.

"No," she whispered harshly and stopped, awestruck.

Kyle looked so handsome, standing next to her. In spite of the darkness, his eyes seemed startlingly compelling. Catty realized that in Nefandus his features had altered. Why hadn't she noticed that before?

He stared back at her with longing, seemingly overcome with emotion. "You look different, too, Catty," he said. "Dangerously beautiful."

She eased closer, putting her hands on his hips, his jeans rough against her palms. Fear heightened her desire for his kiss. "Please," she whispered, willing his head to bend down to hers.

"We'd better hurry." He grasped her hand and started across a gloomy field toward a large lake. A dank, mossy smell grew stronger.

Willow trees lined the banks, their branches brushing lazily over the water. Crickets chirped, and night birds sang, in ghostly imitation of earth's nocturnal songs.

Kyle led her onto a wharf. Their footsteps pounded hollowly.

A small boat bobbed at the end of the dock, its elegantly carved prow surging above the water. A tiny lantern swung from the tip. The flame inside burned lavender. Within the small vessel, a stout man sat stone-still, his face hidden in the shadow of a hood. His large hands rested on the oars.

"Grab on to his robe before you let go of me," Kyle warned as he helped her down a small ladder and into the boat.

She stepped on board and turned back. "Aren't you coming?"

"You're safe," Kyle reassured her. "I'll wait here for you."

Catty settled on the plank seat, then grasped the hem of the man's robe as she released Kyle's hand. He untied the rope from the piling and threw it on the deck.

Without speaking the man rowed out, the oars lapping the water with a soothing, soft rhythm. Soon the boat drifted into a bed of pink lotus blossoms; the air was heavy with their pungent fragrance. The broad, rounded leaves brushed against the hull of the boat.

The monk stopped rowing, and the boat tipped gently back and forth. He took a lantern and set it on the middle seat. Sparks shot from his fingertips, lighting a purple flame inside the glass, and then, slowly, he removed his hood.

Catty inhaled sharply and stared into the face of her father.

CHAPTER TWENTY-THREE

A GASP ESCAPED CATTY'S lips, and she looked at her father with respect. "You're the monk." Hope rose inside her, making her dizzy with happiness. She gripped the side of the boat, using her free hand to brace herself. Warm waves washed over the tips of her fingers.

"I'm not that treasonous monk," her father said harshly. "I was forced into this stupid charade to convince Kyle to bring you to me again."

"You're not . . . then, why . . . ?" Panic seized her, and she sat back, clutching her hands to her chest, expecting Regulators to bob up from the lake and pull her overboard.

When she dropped her hold on the robe, the landscape shifted back to the bewildering clouds. Cold penetrated her skin, and she began to shiver, teeth chattering, fearful she would be imprisoned in the frigid mists again.

"Use your power!" her father scolded, the force of his voice scattering the vapors.

"My powers don't work here," she shouted back, sensing his eyes on her but unable to see him in the murky haze.

"The ones you inherited from me do," he yelled as he locked his icy fingers around her wrist.

The fog vanished, and her father's face came back into fierce focus. His thinning hair seemed alive, writhing snakelike about his head as if expressing his anger, his eyes no longer gentle but dangerous, sly, and spellbinding.

She flinched at the needle-like feel of his thoughts sliding into her head, but she was prepared this time and barred his mental hold. She breathed deeply, summoning all her strength to fight him.

His grip tightened in response, sending a spasm of energy through her blood.

"You're not an outsider, Catty," he said with commanding force. "You can see in Nefandus without my help."

"I can't," she yelled back, glaring at him in anger.

"Stop suppressing your evil," he ordered, and took his hand away.

The foggy landscape returned, but the bitterly cold clouds didn't concern her this time. She was struggling to hold back the primitive force building inside her. She could feel it pacing, testing her control. Her father's touch had awakened her evil birthright. She had always sensed it deep within her, waiting, but now it became restless, pulsing with an ancient rhythm and demanding release.

At last it broke free, raw and excited, consuming her with savage need. Silver light shimmered over the haze. The clouds evaporated, and Nefandus burst back, vivid and clear.

A breeze whispered across the lake, tickling her skin and bringing with it the sweet fragrance of night. Croaking frogs circled the shore, and even though her eyes could not see the tiny amphibians, her mental vision caught each bulging eye and webbed foot.

She felt the predator inside her growing strong and dangerous, and if she leaned back, she knew she could release her body and become a phantom shadow gliding sinuously beneath the willow trees, hunting like a fox. The desire to do so grew inside her, but she was afraid that if she gave in to the impulse, she would never return to what she had been born to be, a goddess. She sat motionless, tears welling up in her eyes, and dug her fingers into the bench, straining against the new urges.

Suddenly her moon amulet felt too heavy to wear. Her hand twitched as if, with a will of its own, it wanted to tear the talisman from her neck and throw it into the still, black waters. Her amulet began to thrum as if it sensed her intention, its power seeping into her, fighting those she had inherited from her father.

"Now you understand what you are," he said.

"I'm also a Daughter," she answered in a slow, silky voice that didn't feel like her own.

"Your mother was a fallen goddess," he said, as if he were proud of the fact. "That trait also resides within you."

"I've vowed to destroy the evil you worship." But even as she spoke, she felt an unbearable pressure to give in, join her father, and align herself with the Atrox.

Her father smiled, his eyes fiery with satisfaction, as if he had already won. "All this time you've been hunting evil, and all you ever had to do was look in the mirror to find it."

"I'm here to protect my world from your kind," she argued.

"My kind?" He waved his hand through the water, guiding the boat deeper into the lotus flowers. Then he pulled a red-lacquered canister and a brass teakettle from under the middle seat and set them next to the lantern. "Perhaps you find it so easy to fight Followers and Regulators because you're really fighting what you know exists inside you. I think we sometimes see ourselves most clearly if we look at what we hate in other people."

She nodded with understanding, but another worry had settled over her. She needed to leave Nefandus before her willpower abandoned her and she remained stuck there forever. "Why did you send for me?" she asked abruptly.

"I need your help." He opened the red canister, and the rich scent of tea leaves filled the air between them. "I have a favor to ask."

"And if I refuse you'll call the Regulators again," she remarked matter-of-factly.

"I didn't call the Regulators the last time you visited me." He leaned over the side of the boat and grasped a flower, then gently opened the lotus bud, pinched tea from the canister, and dropped it inside the blossom.

"Right," she answered, not believing him.

"Do you think you had the power to escape the Regulators without my help?" He pulled a red ribbon from his sleeve and tied the flower shut.

She didn't answer, but she sensed he was telling the truth. Her goddess power didn't work in Nefandus, but why would he help her and risk displeasing the Atrox?

"I manipulated the Regulator's mind to loosen his grip." Her father placed his hand in the water and guided the boat to the next flower.

"And why would you do that?" Catty still couldn't bring herself to trust him completely. "Besides, I broke loose on my own."

"You don't believe me. You think you did it with your prayer?" He stared at her as if her stubbornness fascinated him. "Would my *servus* have helped you to escape without being ordered to do so by me?"

Catty hesitated. "Then why didn't he help me leave Nefandus?"

"You weren't supposed to panic and run," he said "I had assumed you were braver."

"I'm brave enough," she answered, swallowing hard. She needed to hurry. Her evil inheritance was becoming stronger than her will to hold it back, and she knew intuitively it would be easier to control in earth's realm.

Her father glanced at her as if he enjoyed her struggle, then tossed the last bit of tea into a flower and tied it shut. The ribbon's ends dangled in the water.

"By dawn the scent of the lotus flower will have permeated the tea leaves. I'll brew you a cup. Now, help me gather the dew for our water." He folded a leaf, letting the dew flow into the teakettle.

Catty understood at once. Her father was trying to keep her here until her dark side overcame her goddess energy. She glanced at the shore. She could swim the distance, but what creatures lay beneath the glossy surface? She stared at the water, determined to dive in if he stalled any longer. "What favor do you need from me?"

Her father frowned, as if he had grasped her resolve. "I want you to bring me the Scroll."

She smiled, at last understanding. "So you can win a place beside the Atrox?"

"I have that already. Look deeper," he challenged.

She studied his eyes and knew. "You want to replace the Atrox."

"With you beside me," he whispered.

"Never. There's nothing you can do to convince me to surrender the Scroll to you."

"Nothing?" Her father seemed amused. "If you still care for the Keeper, then you'll do as I say."

Her stomach clenched. "Do you know where Chris is?"

He waved his hand, and white smoke hissed into the air. A perfect image of Chris formed in the thick haze. His hair looked longer than the last time Catty had seen him, and he had the haunted look of someone who was unbearably tired. Her heart ached for him.

"Chris!" She jumped up, rocking the boat. Water rushed over the sides, soaking through her sneakers.

Her father continued rowing with a soft, slow rhythm, moving her away from the likeness of Chris. "Unless you bring me the Scroll, he will remain here, my slave."

"Chris!" she shouted again.

Suddenly, Chris looked around as if he had heard her. "Catty, where are you? There's something important I need to tell you."

But then Chris's image fell apart, cascading through the air like fine sand.

She slumped back into her seat, defeated. "Where is he?"

"Safely imprisoned in my home, bound by magic." Her father stopped rowing, and the boat continued to drift forward, then bumped softly into a piling.

"I'll bring you the Scroll." She looked up, expecting to see Kyle waiting for her on the wharf, but he was not there.

Abruptly, the darkness shifted, and instinct told her that Regulators were near.

"Careful," her father whispered, as if he also sensed their approach. "Don't do anything foolish."

But Catty had no intention of waiting passively to see what would happen next. She grabbed on to the first rung of the ladder and climbed up, hoping to run and hide beneath the willow trees before the Regulators could catch her. She bounded onto the dock, took two strides, and began to sprint, her feet pounding, arms pumping at her sides.

The night trembled around her. Shadows gathered and grew denser. Veins of electricity crackled over the churning darkness. She dashed through the twirling shadows. A hand shot out and grabbed her neck, fingers dripping a foul slime down her throat. Within seconds a Regulator formed, connecting to the arm.

Her breath caught, strangling her scream. She glanced back. Her father stood at the end of the pier, still dressed like a monk. What would happen if the Regulators thought he was the one who had been helping the *servi* escape? Maybe Kyle had deceived them both after all.

CHAPTER TWENTY-FOUR

SUDDENLY, THE REGULATOR dropped Catty and stepped over her, stumbling back and joining the others.

Catty landed on her stomach and lay sprawled on the splintered wood, dazed and breathing in the scent of the tar-brushed beams. Cautiously she touched her neck. The liquid clinging to her skin felt like warm honey. She grabbed the edge of her sweater and wiped the mucus away, her stomach churning with nausea. Then she glanced up, looking for a way to flee.

Regulators stood behind her in a solid wall, hovering together, terror distorting their terrible faces. She wondered what had frightened them; then she saw, and her heart skipped a beat.

Her father loomed over them, grinning. He squinted in concentration, and the night thrummed with his energy. Without warning his arm shot out, and he hurled a burst of power at them.

The Regulators shrieked, their hellish cries resounding in the air. Their bodies wiggled and squirmed, trying to break free and transform themselves into shadows, but the force circled them, tightening. Their mangled bodies writhed, their ogreish faces twisted in pain, and then their eyes went hollow and dead. They froze, lifeless—half-shadow, half-freak.

Catty's breath stopped, unable to grasp what she had just witnessed.

Her father grinned triumphantly and

stepped forward. He paused in front of the Regulators' silent forms. In the odd light, his features looked barbaric and cruel, his cheekbones sharp, and his thin smile ruthless.

"Stupid beasts," he muttered, not bothering to hide his contempt. He whistled, and they vanished.

Catty knew intuitively that every trace of them had been destroyed. Fear leaped through her. Her father's strength was astonishing. She smoothed her trembling hand over the place where the Regulators had stood moments before. It still felt warm. She glanced back at her father, and the joy on his face made her queasy.

Her nerves were taut with the need to jump up and run, but she continued to stare at him, wondering what evil he had committed in order to receive such power. It was greater than any she had witnessed before. Was this her heritage? Part of her longed to embrace his magic, but a stronger part felt terrified by what she had witnessed.

Her father seemed to sense her fear. "Leave now, and bring me the Scroll."

Still she hesitated. Even if she brought him the Scroll, she had no guarantee that he would release Chris.

"Go quickly," her father urged. "You have only minutes before the door between the worlds closes, and if you stay, I have no promise of your safety. The Atrox will soon discover that five of its Regulators have vanished, and you'll be suspected, not I."

"Three days have passed already?" she asked.

"Must you always question everything?" His fingers trembled as if power were building in his hands. "Go, before I lose my patience."

Catty pulled herself slowly to her feet and took an awkward step backward. Her legs felt too shaky to hold her.

"Hurry," he yelled, a scowl creasing his forehead. "Do you want to be trapped here?"

Obediently she turned and ran clumsily beneath the long line of willow trees, the branches brushing against her face. She turned and darted across the field, clutching her moon amulet for encouragement. The dew on the grass wet her ankles, and she slipped but continued forward, scrambling on her hands and knees up the steepest part of the hill, wanting nothing more than to be safely back in earth's realm. She kept picturing her friends and her mother, knowing that if she thought about how far she had to go to get home, she would break down and cry.

Soon, the grinding music of unfamiliar instruments burst into the air. She rushed along the flowering bushes, to the edge of the park, then darted down the cobblestone road, staying clear of shadows, fearing what might be lurking in the dark.

At last, she turned the corner and saw the portal in front of her, but footsteps pounded behind her. Immediately she changed direction and started up another path back into the park, hoping the person behind her was only a *servus* out on an errand.

She lunged forward, muscles straining.

Shadows spread across the field, trees bending in a cold breeze. Leaves tumbled about, clinging to her jeans and sweater. She glanced over her shoulder, frantically trying to see behind her, but a sudden gust blew her hair into her eyes. The trailing footfalls sounded again. Whoever was chasing after her was closing the gap between them. She tried to quiet her fears and concentrated on getting home.

At last she sped up another hill, heading for the cliff, and trying desperately to remember the point from which she had jumped before.

Something tramped in the grass behind her, gaining on her. This time she didn't glance back to see who was after her. Turning around even briefly would have slowed her pace, and she was too close now. She surged forward, arms and legs thrashing, then hit the air hard and screamed, her stomach lurching as she tumbled downward at an impossible speed. Had she leaped from the wrong place?

Wind lashed against her, ripping the air from her lungs. Then everything stopped. Silence surrounded her, and the filmy membrane locked itself about her. She gasped for air, but before she could breathe, her body became deadened, paralyzed as before.

Slow pain finally awakened her senses, and she rolled forward, stumbling into Los Angeles in the middle of Chinatown. Catty started to lean against the wall and to gaze up at the moon and the crystal-white stars, grateful to be back home.

Suddenly, something pushed against her back, and someone broke through the brick wall, joining her in this world.

CHAPTER TWENTY-FIVE

"CATTY, DIDN'T YOU HEAR me calling you?" Kyle stepped through the portal and joined her, his breath coming in gasps, hair falling into his eyes.

"You were the one chasing me?" The tension in her back eased, and she rested her cheek against his chest, relieved to see him.

He placed his arms around her. "As soon as

I realized your father had deceived me, I hid. I figured Regulators were going to show up, and I'd need to rescue you, but your father—"

Kyle stopped as if the memory of what he had seen had come back to him unexpectedly and in horrifying detail. "I've never seen anyone destroy Regulators so easily," he continued finally.

"I know." She pulled away from him and started toward his car.

The winds had settled, and quiet claimed the night. People were out enjoying the clear skies.

"Do you know another way to get into Nefandus?" Catty asked, feeling the pressure of time. Chris hadn't seemed well, and she didn't know how much longer he could survive.

"Just because you're able to see in Nefandus now doesn't mean it's safe for you to go back there," Kyle warned.

"You go in and out all the time," Catty said, wishing she had Vanessa's power to become invisible and fly home on the wind.

"I'm cautious," he answered, then continued, "You don't understand. Too many will sense your presence if you go there, and you won't have your father or me to protect you."

She cocked her head in a flirty way, trying to convince him. "Just take me home. Besides, if I have the Scroll with me I'll be okay."

"You won't be," he said, his eyes filled with apprehension.

A dark foreboding rushed through her, and even though the night was warm, she began to shiver.

"Chris has always known what his fate would be if Followers captured him," Kyle said softly. "We all know."

"You don't understand." Catty turned and started back toward the street. "I don't have a choice. I'm a Daughter. I have to try."

"You might save him," Kyle said, trailing behind her, "but at a terrible price."

"I can't just forget him," she argued. "If I leave him in Nefandus, then I'm no better than my father."

"You're not your father." Kyle grabbed her arm and pulled her back. "You were given the

Scroll, and it can only be given to someone with a pure heart and the strength to fight the Atrox."

She looked down at the sidewalk so he couldn't see the tears brimming in her eyes. She didn't feel like the legitimate heir. Primal forces were working inside her, prowling around in her heart and mind, waiting for an opportunity to attack and claim her. Others had used the Scroll, so what made everyone so sure she was the rightful heir? She glanced at the moon, watching it through tear-blurred vision, and issued a silent prayer for guidance.

"I have to do it," she whispered finally.

"You can't, Catty," Kyle said. "It's a trick, to capture you and the Scroll."

"You don't know that for sure," she argued, wiping her eyes. She didn't need him to raise any more doubts; she had enough of her own. "And what if Chris needs me? Maybe my destiny is to save him." A tense silence hung between them. "Are you jealous of Chris?" she asked brazenly. "Is that the real reason you're so upset and trying to talk me out of going back to Nefandus?"

"I'm not jealous of Chris," he answered, his face stone still. "And if you knew the truth, you'd know it's impossible for me to feel jealous of him."

Catty studied Kyle. "I need time to be alone and think." The words came from her mouth before she was even aware that she was going to say them. "I'll catch a bus and call you when I get home."

He nodded, not bothering to hide his hurt. "But promise you won't go back to Nefandus. At least not until after you talk to me again."

"I promise," she answered, protecting her thoughts the way she sometimes had to do when she was around Serena.

Kyle seemed reluctant to leave her. "You're sure?"

She smiled, trying to keep her mind blank, and shrugged prettily. "I have three days before I can even go back to Nefandus," she answered. "I'll call you tomorrow."

He waved, and she watched him walk away.

CHAPTER TWENTY-SIX

A BLAST OF SMALL explosions startled Catty. She whirled, her heart racing, and knocked into a dowdy old woman. A fiery dragon was embroidered on the front of her blouse.

"It's all right." The woman grinned, revealing gold-capped teeth. "The boys are setting off firecrackers to scare away bad luck. The noise frightens evil spirits."

A boy lit a fuse and threw a string of firecrackers. Sparks shot forth, and a series of bangs crackled in the air.

Catty stuck her fingers into her ears. Tendrils of thin smoke writhed into her nose, bitter and stinging. Above her a large banner flapped lazily, announcing the grand opening of the Summer Moon Tea Room.

"Come in." The woman in the dragon blouse ushered Catty inside the narrow restaurant between a grocery store and a curio shop. "I'll fix you my specialty."

"I really have to leave." Catty started to protest, but the woman seized her wrist with bony fingers and pulled her past the crowded tables to a corner booth.

"This is where you're supposed to be." The woman smiled mysteriously and disappeared behind the counter.

Catty looked around, breathing in the savory aromas coming from a wok, then hurried down a hallway to the back, looking for the bathroom. A pay phone hung on the wall between two doors. She fished two coins from her pockets, dropped them into the slot, and punched in a number.

"Hello?" Vanessa answered.

Catty's chin began to quiver, her body ready to break into sobs. She hadn't anticipated having such a strong reaction to hearing her best friend's voice.

"Catty?" Vanessa said in a worried tone.

"Vanessa," Catty sniffled.

"What's wrong?" Vanessa asked, her voice rising to panic.

"Everything." Catty shielded her face with her hand so the patrons approaching the restrooms wouldn't see her red eyes. Then she quickly told Vanessa what had happened, starting with Kyle and ending with Nefandus and her father.

"Where are you now?" Vanessa asked when she had finished.

"In Chinatown." Catty wiped her nose on her sweater sleeve. "The Summer Moon Tea Room. It's a new place."

"Stay put," Vanessa instructed. "I'll get the Scroll and pick up the others. We'll be there in no time."

"Don't get the Scroll!" Catty shouted, but Vanessa had already hung up.

Catty dropped the receiver into its cradle, then rushed into the restroom, locking the door behind her. She washed up with cold water, harsh soap, and rough paper towels, then sauntered back into the tea room, looking like a runaway. She slipped into the booth, and the waitress returned with a tray.

"This will soothe you," the waitress said. She tipped the kettle, and steam rose from the spout, curling around Catty with the delicate fragrance of jasmine tea.

"Thank you," Catty said, her voice breaking; the woman's kindness made her want to cry again.

"Animis non astutia," the woman whispered.

Catty's head shot up. "Did you just speak Latin?"

"Did I?" The woman set an array of food and sauces on the table.

Catty nodded, certain of what she had heard. "You said, 'By courage, not by cunning.'"

The waitress shrugged. "It sounds like good advice for anyone who wants to triumph over impossible odds."

Then she handed Catty a single fortune cookie on a silver plate with the changing shapes of the moon engraved on its border.

"Don't forget to read your fortune," she said and took her tray to a nearby table to clear the dirty dishes there.

Catty dipped a meat-filled dumpling into tangy vinegar sauce and took a bite. Sharp, spicy flavors burst into her mouth. Only then did she realize how hungry she had become. She ate, staring at the dragons and cranes emblazoned on the walls, and listened to the murmured conversations around her.

At last, she snapped open her cookie and started to read the fortune, but a rasping cough made her look up.

Vanessa had just entered, her face flushed, hair disheveled, a huge, pink purse slung over her shoulder. She wore silky cargo pants, a beaded top, and intense, dark, eye shadow painted to the outside corner of her eyes.

Catty slipped the fortune into her jean pocket unread and waved. She wondered if Vanessa had been working on a new look for her next performance when she had called.

Vanessa saw her, sneezed into a tissue, and began squeezing between the tables, heading towards Catty.

Serena followed, wearing a swirling black skirt, lace nylons, and combat boots. Her moon-and-star earrings dangled to her shoulders.

Tianna stumbled close behind, still dressed in flannel PJs. A yellow woolen scarf was tossed haphazardly around her neck. Her untied shoe-laces trailed from her purple, high-top sneakers.

Conversation paused, and the diners looked up, watching the girls walk past them.

Vanessa handed Catty the purse and coughed again. "Here," she said, hoarsely.

"How'd you get the Scroll?" Catty didn't need to look inside to know it was there. She could feel it pulsing through the fabric, greeting her.

"She went invisible and got it from your bedroom." Serena leaned over the table, snatched a dumpling from Catty's plate, and popped it into her mouth.

"Can you imagine what kind of guts that took after what happened in the museum?" Tianna asked, scooting in next to Serena.

Vanessa shrugged and slid into the booth as if it were nothing.

"You were able to make it invisible this time?" Catty asked, moving over to make room.

Vanessa gave her a funny look. "The Scroll was eager to go with me," she said uneasily. "It purred like a cat when I picked it up."

Tianna held up her hand in warning, and they stopped talking while a kid in a black, hooded sweatshirt and baggy jeans walked past them and slouched into an adjoining booth.

"You took a big risk." Catty poured Vanessa a cup of tea and handed it to her. "The curse—"

"What else could I do?" Vanessa pulled an aspirin tin from her pocket, tossed two pills into her mouth, then swallowed some tea. "You said

Chris looked like he was dying, so I got the Scroll in case you'd figured out another way to get back to your father."

"Do you think we can trust your father to surrender Chris if we do give him the Scroll?" Tianna asked.

"No," Catty said, sadly.

"Then maybe we should just go in and get Chris out before your father even knows we're there," Tianna suggested.

"We'd still have to wait until the portal opens." Catty felt her anxiety rising. "I don't know if Chris can survive that long."

"You said it was the same place where you'd been imprisoned," Serena said, wiping her fingers on a napkin.

Catty nodded. "Only, now, I can see past the fog."

"So what about Tianna?" Serena asked. "She used her telekinetic powers to get us inside when we rescued you. Maybe she can do it again."

Catty looked at Tianna, remembering how she had lifted the veil between the two worlds once before. "Do you think you can?"

"What if someone sees us disappear?" Vanessa asked, apprehensively looking around.

"It's too dark," Serena reassured her. "No one's going to see." She nudged Tianna. "Go ahead."

"I'll try, but my powers are still pretty messed up from my fall." Tianna rubbed her shoulder as if it were tender.

"What's wrong?" Catty asked.

"The last time we went there the Atrox was waiting for us." Tianna's eyes widened with uneasiness.

"But it was using Catty as a lure." Serena clicked her tongue ring impatiently against her teeth. "How will it know we're coming this time?"

"It's a chance we have to take," Vanessa said bravely. "Besides, I want to see what Nefandus really looks like."

"Then don't let go of me once we're inside," Catty warned. "You'll need to hold on to me to be able to see more than mists."

"Ready?" Tianna squinted in concentration, her energy building.

The table began to quiver. Then the floor trembled. The front window buckled. A crack shattered the wall, and wooden beams popped.

"Earthquake!" someone screamed, and others joined in.

An earsplitting roar filled the tea room, and pandemonium broke loose. Diners dove under tables, spilling tea and water. Dishes crashed to the floor.

"Stop!" Catty shouted, bracing herself against the back of the booth. "You're wrecking the place."

Tianna looked up, her eyes bloodshot, and the movement stopped.

Vanessa clapped her hand over her mouth and tried to stop giggling. "I'm sorry," she said at last. "I know it's not funny, but usually I'm the one who messes up this badly."

Tianna scowled. "I can do it. Let me try again."

"Lucky for us this is earthquake country,"

Serena put in and set a bottle of soy sauce upright.

Diners began peeking out from under their tables. Spilled soup dripped to the floor, and a small fire had started near the wok.

"Jeez, I made a mess of everything," Tianna muttered. "Maybe I should fix it before we leave."

"Not now," Catty warned. "You might make it worse."

Tianna shot her an angry look.

"After Nefandus, we'll come back and make repairs." Serena took Tianna's hand. "Let's combine powers."

"Try again," Vanessa agreed and grasped Tianna's wrist.

Catty slung the purse over her shoulder and grabbed Tianna's arm. Immediately power flowed from her fingers, seeping into Tianna.

Then the room swayed, the air undulating. This time the diners didn't notice anything unusual. The change was affecting only Catty and her friends. The wall in their booth wavered, the painted dragons and cranes seeming to take flight.

At last the restaurant broke in two with a deafening boom, and they were swept into Nefandus, the violent force separating them.

Catty thrashed about, trying to find her friends and grab on to them.

She plunged downward, her stomach lurching, and didn't feel the strange numbness she had experienced before. No comforting membrane stopped her fall this time. The passing was unlike the others, and terrifying.

Maybe it was a trap, after all. Was that what Kyle had been trying to tell her? Perhaps her father had known all along that she would return with her friends and try to rescue Chris.

Now he would have all four Daughters of the Moon *and* the Scroll.

CHAPTER TWENTY-SEVEN

CATTY LANDED ON HER feet with a sharp jolt. Her back hit a rocky outcropping, and piercing pain shot up her spine. She stood, catching her breath, and slowly realized she was balanced precariously on a narrow ledge. She swung her hands back, trying to clutch the mountain face, feeling dizzy from the high elevation.

The Scroll pulsed excitedly against her, its hum joining the fast rhythm of her heart.

"I only see fog and clouds, like before," Vanessa said with accusation.

"Because you're not holding on to me." Catty looked around but didn't see Vanessa. "Where are you?"

"Here," three voices answered.

Catty glanced up, and caught her breath.

Vanessa and Tianna floated in the air, dazed expressions on their faces, as if they were lost in the mists, but Serena did a somersault, oblivious to the danger, and dived toward the jagged rocks below, her arms spread wide.

"This is exactly what I remember from last time!" Serena shouted.

"Stop!" Catty screamed, unable to watch. Then, in a calmer tone, she added, "Follow the sound of my voice."

When she opened her eyes again, Vanessa, Tianna, and Serena were drifting sluggishly toward her like inexperienced swimmers thrashing and straining against a riptide.

In a few minutes, Vanessa hovered inches above her.

Catty caught her hand and tugged hard.

Vanessa fell against the cliff, scraping her cheek. Pebbles and dirt rained over her. She staggered, then whipped around and cried out, her fingernails digging into Catty's palm.

"I liked it better when I couldn't see," Vanessa said, sounding fearful.

"We entered from a different location," Catty explained. "You can see the city in the distance."

Then Catty jumped, seized Serena's arm, and yanked on it strenuously.

Serena shrieked and crashed on top of them. They sprawled helplessly on the narrow ledge, Catty's legs hanging over the edge, the Scroll quivering, sensing new danger.

Carefully, they stood, helping one another up.

"The air felt as thick as water before," Serena said, waving her free hand in front of her. "Now it feels normal. What gives?"

"It seems like there's some strange connection between vision and gravity here," Catty explained.

"How?" Vanessa asked, leaning back against the cliff.

"Magic," Tianna answered. "I'm pretty sure the air is like a spiderweb that stops people who don't belong."

Catty looked over her shoulder, dumbfounded.

Tianna stood, wedged up beside her, her fingers resting on Catty's shoulder.

"How did you find us?" Catty asked.

"I didn't," Tianna went on. "I knocked into something solid, and then suddenly I landed here beside you."

Catty felt certain Tianna hadn't been touching her when she first spoke, but before she could question her, Vanessa did.

"What do you mean, like a spiderweb?" Vanessa asked.

"It's a way to catch trespassers," Tianna went on. "Someone who doesn't belong here only sees the mists and flounders about like a fly struggling on a spiderweb. Just as the vibrations tell the spider that dinner has landed, an intruder disturbs the air and alerts the Atrox or its Regulators that an outsider has stumbled into Nefandus."

"How do you know that?" Catty asked.

Tianna shrugged. "I don't," she answered simply. "I'm assuming, from what happened before."

"Bizarro mundo," a familiar voice said in Spanglish.

"Jimena?" Catty cranked her head around and looked up.

Jimena sat perched above them, wedged between massive boulders, the hood of her black sweatshirt resting around her neck.

Serena grabbed Jimena's ankle, and a startled look crossed Jimena's face. "What the—?" She glanced down. "Where are we?"

"In Nefandus," Catty said. "How did you get in here?"

"I don't know." Jimena shook her head, her eyes wide with wonder.

"But you must have done something," Serena

said, clutching Jimena tightly as she climbed down and joined them on the ledge.

"I've been following you guys since that night at the museum," Jimena explained. "Trying to keep you out of more trouble." She frowned, as if she were working through her recent memories, searching for the right one. Then she continued, "I was in the tea room, yelling for you to get under the table. Then the *temblores* stopped and you started talking like you had made the earthquake. The next thing I know, I'm in this dreamworld."

"We have to tell her the truth," Serena said.

"Not without Maggie's permission," Vanessa argued. "She's not supposed to know what she once was."

"What was I?" Jimena whispered.

"Now you've done it." Serena glared at Vanessa. "Are you still not going to tell her?"

"You were a goddess," Catty said softly, ignoring Vanessa's piercing stare. "A Daughter of the Moon."

Jimena was silent for a long time, struggling

to hold back the tears brimming in her eyes. Finally, she spoke. "My *abuelita* keeps telling me that I told her I was *una diosa,* a goddess, on my last birthday. I just thought she was getting old and imagining things."

"That's the day you lost your memory of being a Daughter," Serena explained. "So, if you did tell her, you wouldn't remember doing it."

Jimena wiped at her tears with her sleeve, her voice barely audible. "Strange memories have been coming back to me."

"You remember being a goddess?" Catty asked, baffled.

Jimena shook her head and touched the Medusa stone hanging around her neck as if she were seeking comfort. "It's like I'm still me, but I'm also becoming someone else."

Catty stared at her. "What do you mean?"

Jimena shrugged. "I think I've lived a lot of lives before this one."

"I wish Maggie were here," Vanessa whispered.

"Who's Maggie?" Jimena asked.

"It doesn't matter." Serena smiled sympathetically. "We'll tell you everything we know."

They started off single file down the rocky path, clasping hands and taking turns telling Jimena about her past.

By the time they reached the city, the sun had vanished, and a strange silence had settled over them. Their footsteps were the only sounds breaking the quiet. Catty led them down an alley, keeping close to the buildings. The gargoyles perched on the steeply pitched roofs cast night shadows across the cobblestones.

"Where is everyone?" Serena asked. "It's like a ghost town."

"They're following us," Jimena said simply.

"What?" Catty turned, her palms sweating from clutching Vanessa and Serena's hands so tightly. The passage between the tall houses looked empty behind her.

"Don't turn your head," Jimena whispered. "Act like you're looking in front of you, and check it out from the corner of your eye."

Catty walked a few more steps and tried

again. She cast a sideways glance and caught stealthy movement. Shadows swayed restlessly beneath the trees. Heavy, dark forms billowed, then vanished, only to reappear closer, watching with evil intent.

"What do you think they are?" Vanessa asked.

"Regulators," Serena whispered nervously. "They're following us, but why aren't they attacking?"

"Our powers don't work here," Catty added. "So there's no reason for them to hesitate."

"Unless they have orders," Tianna suggested. "Maybe they're protecting us."

Catty shivered. "Why would they?"

"You said your father was powerful," Tianna answered in a low voice. "So he must have enemies, Followers who don't want him to have the Scroll. Maybe these shadows are his sentinels, making sure we get to him safely."

"If he knows we're here, that is," Catty answered, praying that he didn't. She wanted to get Chris and take him back to earth's realm before her father was even aware that she had come back to Nefandus.

"Can you imagine Regulators protecting us?" Vanessa asked with a dry laugh.

A minute later they stood across the street from Catty's father's home. Lanterns suspended from iron brackets swung overhead. Sparks shot from the flames, and the red embers swirled around them, mixing a sweet, smoldering aroma into the air.

Catty pressed back against a stone wall, her nerves tingling, and stared at the jade dragons on either side of the huge door. Fires blazed from their ferocious jaws, casting light across the veranda. The demons in the stained-glass windows seemed alive, slinking back and forth in the firelight as if they were guarding the front entrance. Overhead, bluish smoke from the hearth fire spiraled out from the chimney, changing from one phantom form to another.

"How are we going to get inside without your father knowing?" Jimena asked.

Catty shook her head, feeling defeated

already. Kyle was right. She was too impetuous, too careless, and now she had brought her friends into danger.

"Let's check out the back," she whispered boldly, and she started forward, forcing her legs to move, her body rebelling against each step. The Scroll rested silently against her, as if the nearness to her father had hushed it.

"We need to hurry," Serena cautioned.

The air seemed suddenly filled with furtive murmurings.

"Something's happening." Vanessa inhaled sharply and looked around.

Catty felt it, too, an abrupt change, like a sudden drop in air pressure.

"There," Jimena whispered, pointing upward.

Raven-black clouds gathered above them, but the thunderheads didn't look as if they were heralding a storm.

"Is it the Atrox?" Tianna whispered, her voice tense with fear.

"I don't think so," Catty answered.

Sudden terror rushed through her, and

sickening memories poured into her, as if from a primitive consciousness she shared with her evil forebears. She knew at once that within the cloud was a Follower, a powerful member of the Inner Circle, who was also her father's enemy, and thus her own.

Immediately she understood, as if the Follower's intentions had been sent to her by some low-grade telepathy. The Follower intended to sacrifice all four Daughters and gain their power. Their blood would give him access to the energy he needed to destroy her father. But who had let him know of their arrival? Her mind quickly turned to Kyle. Had he been trying to warn her of this, or had he read her mind and understood even better than she did her rash impetuous behavior, and how easy it would be for him to deceive her and set this trap?

Without warning the cloud shrieked down on them.

Catty bolted forward. "Go!" she yelled, and ran jerkily, pulling her friends behind her. "Run faster."

Only moments before, Catty had hoped her father wouldn't discover her presence in Nefandus. Now she prayed that he was waiting for her. She needed his protection. On her own, she didn't have the strength to banish the Follower roaring down on them.

The storm grew stronger, beating around them in a frenzy of spinning winds, trying to keep them from reaching her father's home.

The distance to the huge house now seemed impossibly wide.

CHAPTER TWENTY-EIGHT

CATTY SPRINTED FORWARD, deliberately ignoring the road leading up to the veranda. She cut across at a diagonal to the darker side of the house and ran haphazardly through the thorny bushes. Her friends tromped behind her, gasping and wheezing.

"What are you doing?" Vanessa screamed. "The door's the other way."

"Such a huge place has to have a basement," Catty answered. "If we can find a bottom window, we can break through and slide inside."

The demon black shadow swirled about in anger and closed tightly, stealing her breath. Winds twisted the brambles around her, snagging her sweater and hair.

Vanessa cried out as a thorn slashed her face.

"There!" Serena shouted, pointing to the base of the house.

A prickly vine wrapped around Catty's arm. She yanked free, her skin stinging with scratches, and retraced her steps. Her breath came in labored huffs by the time she stopped in front of the dirt-streaked window. She kicked furiously.

"Kick!" she shouted, not sure her friends could even hear her over the howling gusts around them.

Jimena joined her, frantically kicking until the glass shattered and splashed like diamonds falling into the dark below.

With no time to think, Catty flopped onto the ground. Her friends tumbled next to her, scooting closer, as if they were riding a toboggan.

"Ready?" She inched forward until she was balanced on the ledge.

The storm screeched down at her, thrashing against her face with bitter cold and snarling her hair, trying to keep her from jumping.

"Don't let go of me, no matter what!" she shouted, and threw herself into the darkness. She flailed crazily, Serena screaming beside her.

Savage red flames exploded around her, flickering wildly, burning her face and searing her eyebrows. For the briefest moment she thought she was plunging into the depths of hell. She caught the wide-eyed terror on Vanessa's face, then realized that the lantern flames had ignited automatically, as if the girls' presence had made them blaze. Glinting orange light lit the gray dungeon walls. She hit the ground, chin first.

She skidded on her stomach, her hands and shoulders throbbing. Then, she lay still, tasting the blood that trickled into her mouth, and desperately clasped Serena and Vanessa's limp fingers in her hands. She felt too afraid to lift her head, too terrified to ask if her friends were all right.

She blinked to keep tears from her eyes and immediately became aware of her father's protection wrapping itself around her, his power warm and comforting in spite of his vile past.

She lay on a rugged stone floor. Black, muddy dirt oozing up through the cracks with a dank musty stench made her recoil. She wondered vaguely if the smell was the aroma of evil, and she shuddered at the thought.

Abruptly, a crashing sound made her turn. She winced at the pain in her neck.

Wind thrashed against the empty window frame, seeming to shake the foundation but unable to enter her father's home. Stillness followed, and a thin, pallid face stared at her from within a black, roiling cloud. Catty watched in horror as the features became elongated, turning into a twist of night before disappearing.

"Who was that?" Vanessa whispered, leaning against her, her breath coming in agonizing bursts.

"One of my father's enemies—my enemy," Catty choked in a shaky voice as she struggled to sit up.

"Who cares who it was?" Jimena said. "Is it coming back?"

"I don't think so," Catty answered, feeling that this was true but not understanding the reason why. "How is everyone?"

"As well as can be expected," Serena answered bluntly. Her skirt was torn, and a purple bruise swelled on her cheekbone. "Can't we ever do anything the easy way?"

Hollow footsteps pounded on the floorboards overhead, and the girls froze.

"Do you think your father heard us?" Tianna whispered. Her scarf was gone, and two buttons were missing from her pajama top.

"No, it has to be one of his *servi*," Catty said. "I'm certain he isn't home. If he were, he would have engaged the Follower in the storm cloud."

"*¡Orale!*" Jimena nodded, her hand swelling as if it had broken. "He wouldn't let his *enemigo* come into his territory like that."

"Let's get on with it." Vanessa started to stand, then moaned and stretched in a rolling motion, slow and careful. "This place is creeping me out."

Catty stood, also eager to leave, and looked around the gloomy cellar, searching for a door or stairs. When she didn't see a way out, she began to panic. Then she saw Jimena staring at something and followed her gaze.

Flat stones were lodged into the wall, almost invisible in the strange light from the lantern fires.

"It looks dangerous," Jimena whispered, more to herself than to Catty. She cranked her neck, looking up at the distance they were about to climb.

Catty nodded and started across the chamber, pain exploding in her knees.

A huge door waited at the top of the stairs under a round archway with demon carvings on top. Catty feared her only exit would be locked, but there was no way she could salvage what she had done now. She took another step.

Finally she pushed her shoulder against the

polished wood, and the door eased open with a soft scraping of hinges.

Catty entered a vast hallway and waited for the others to join her. Garishly painted wood carvings of grotesque creatures looked down at them from the ceiling.

"How do you know which way to go?" Serena asked.

"I don't." Catty paused, helplessly lost. Then she became aware of the Scroll vibrating against her with agitated fierceness, as if it were trying to tell her which way to go. "I think the Scroll must sense Chris's presence."

"Are you sure?" Vanessa looked doubtful.

"The Scroll is leading me," Catty answered, feeling both terrified and excited. She hurried down the hall, then started up another flight of stairs, only to pause, sensing a change in the Scroll. It was urging her to continue down the corridor instead. She turned back.

She had only gone a little way when a force greater than she could have imagined pulsed steadily against her, and she knew instinctively that the Scroll was telling her to stop.

"What now?" Jimena asked, looking around.

"I'm not sure." Catty leaned against the wall behind her, considering what to do next, and the wood panel flew open. She stumbled into a dusty stairwell.

Immediately, rusted lanterns flickered on, casting a poor light.

Catty brushed away some gluey cobwebs and started up the twisting stairs, leaving footprints in the dust.

"He can't be up here," Tianna said behind her. "No one has used these steps for centuries."

"Of course they haven't," Serena countered with a snicker. "Most Followers become shadows and fly."

Catty pressed forward more quickly now, feeling the Scroll's energy flutter through her.

At the top of the stairs she came to a door. She held her breath and entered.

Chris sat on a window seat at the far end of the room, gazing out at the darkness as though he were waiting for something. He turned, surprised, blinking in disbelief. He seemed overcome with emotion. Suddenly he scowled.

"Why did you come, Catty?" he asked, his blue eyes filling with anger. "It was a foolish and dangerous thing to try. You'll never escape."

The Scroll throbbed. It wanted to go to Chris.

"I came here because you said you needed to tell me something important," she answered, wondering what held him imprisoned. She didn't see bars, ropes, or chains.

Guilt flashed in his eyes and he looked away from her. "I've failed in my mission, and I must suffer the consequences."

"You haven't failed," she argued, stepping closer. "I have the Scroll, and Tianna can take us back to earth's realm."

"Let's do it now," Tianna said nervously and clasped his hand.

Jimena took his other hand, completing a circle.

Even though their goddess powers didn't work in Nefandus, Tianna had once before lifted the veil between the worlds from inside. Catty hoped she could do it again now.

Tianna gazed at the fireplace behind Catty, her face tense. Her eyes narrowed in tight slits, and her concentration pulsed through the air, her energy becoming stronger.

The walls wrinkled, and Nefandus started to fade away. Then, suddenly, it came back into sharp focus.

Tianna gasped, as if she had been holding her breath. "Something's wrong," she said, frowning. "There's a counterforce working against me."

"You never should have come here," Chris said.

Catty ignored him, not understanding his agitation. She had expected at least a little gratitude. "We'll go to the portal, then," she said, and started toward the door.

"What about the cloud that chased us?" Serena asked, distressed.

"I don't think we need to worry about that right now," Vanessa said, her voice a mix of fear and disgust.

"My guards," Chris said, looking over Catty's shoulder. "I warned you we couldn't escape."

Catty turned and gazed into the misshapen face of a Regulator materializing near her. His hot breath sprayed over her nose and lips. She spit, trying to get the putrid taste out of her mouth.

Only the Regulator's head had formed, resting hideously on circling shadows. His eyes gleamed with triumph, arms and legs still pulling together from floating specks that looked like a cloud of flies.

The air grew blacker, then pulsed as more Regulators formed from slow, lazy swirls. Their fierce power crackled about the room.

Catty stepped backward, pulling the others with her, feeling suddenly powerless and defeated. She held back a childish desire to cry. She had brought all the Daughters to their doom, and there was nothing they could do.

CHAPTER TWENTY-NINE

"JIMENA, USE YOUR Medusa stone!" Catty shouted, suddenly understanding that these creatures weren't Regulators but a spell cast by her father to imprison Chris. "Maybe that will work here." The stone protected against magic and warded off evil spirits.

Jimena looked baffled, but dropped her hold on Chris. Then, still holding on tightly to Serena, she grabbed her amulet and held it up. It glowed fiercely. The snakes carved on it coiled, getting ready to attack. Then twin pools of light streaked from the Gorgon's eyes.

The confused Regulators shrieked and began to shrink, their thick hands shielding their faces from the brightness. They cringed, wincing in pain, then blustered away, howling in defeat. After they were gone, their shrill cries echoed about the small room, then stopped.

But the silence was worse. Catty's neck prickled, and instinct told her to hurry; they were still in grave danger.

"Come on," she whispered. "Let's go to the portal."

Ten minutes later they rushed down a narrow, twisting street, linking hands, their shoes shuffling over the cobblestones. They found a stoop at the back of a dark house and slid onto it together, sheltered by an overhanging balcony on the second floor. A single lantern, with broken panes and a hissing flame, cast a pool of gray light over them.

"I don't think we'll have to wait too long," Catty said.

"How are you going to know when the portal opens?" Vanessa rested her head on the wall behind her.

"We'll sense it," Tianna said with assurance as she leaned back.

Chris stood and ambled over to Catty. "Will you take a walk with me?" he asked, his eyes gazing into hers.

"I can't," she answered, looking at her friends. "They'll be lost in the mists if I leave."

"Go," Vanessa ordered, shaking free of Catty's grip. "We'll stay put."

Serena pulled her hand away and froze as if she were afraid that any movement might send her drifting into the fog that now blinded her to Nefandus.

Catty stood, flexing her fingers, trying to work out the numbness, and stepped beside Chris, feeling awkward to be with him again after so long. He seemed so different from her memories and daydreams.

"I'm sorry, Catty," he said when they reached the corner. "There's so much I should have told you."

"You mean, like showing me that the real steps were hidden within the artwork bordering the Scroll?" She stopped beneath an overhanging wisteria bush, uneasy about going farther away from the portal and her friends.

Chris nervously brushed his hand through the purple flowers, and blossoms fluttered over them. For a moment she thought he was going to kiss her, but then he looked down, as if ashamed. "My duty was to lift the mystery surrounding the Scroll for you."

"Why didn't you?" she asked.

"I failed, because I loved you," he said simply.

She stared at him, wondering why those words didn't excite her as they once would have.

He seemed to understand and touched her cheek tenderly. "The path is dangerous. No one before you has ever survived the first step. They always make a fatal error, and the Atrox takes them. I refused to let you take that risk, and as a result I've only created more problems for you."

"You couldn't help it if Followers captured you and brought you here," she answered, rubbing his arm to let him know she wasn't upset with him.

"You don't understand. I had already lost the Scroll. I didn't want to lose you, too." He sighed heavily. "I came here freely."

"Why?" Catty asked, unable to believe what he was telling her.

"Centuries back I realized the Scroll was becoming too powerful. I was afraid that one day it might have the strength to control the heir, so I added the tenth step."

"That's the only one I couldn't find," Catty said, realizing the Scroll had awakened and seemed to slither against the inside of her purse, intent on listening to their conversation.

"That step is the most important one," he said simply. "But no heir has ever had the courage to follow it."

"Can you tell me what it is?" she asked.

"Later. I have something I need to tell you first, while I still have the courage." He paused, then continued. "I lied when I told you that we could be together some day."

"But you said you had to find a way—"

He pressed his hand gently against her lips to stop her. His fingers chilled her.

"I knew even then it was impossible, because when I added the tenth step to the manuscript, the Scroll bound my life to its existence. That's why I came here. I asked your father to break the spell that binds me to the Scroll, so that you and I could be together."

She inhaled sharply, shocked. "You asked my father to help you, knowing the risk?"

"I wanted to be with you." He tried to take her hand, but she drew away from him.

"Did he make you a Follower?" She felt almost sick. He started to say something more, but before he could, she sensed a mysterious force coming toward them. Shadows seemed to jump everywhere, spreading around her.

"What is it?" he asked.

"I don't know," she said, but suddenly everything felt terribly wrong. She turned abruptly and sprinted back to her friends. Chris raced behind her.

Catty grabbed Serena's hand. Her eyes flashed with fear.

"What happened?" Serena asked, reading the terror on Catty's face. She quickly clasped Jimena's hand.

Jimena looked up, stunned, and glanced around. "Is the gate opening?"

"Something's coming," Catty answered, as she gripped Vanessa's hand.

Vanessa stood up with a jerk, searching for the danger. She seized Tianna by the arm and pulled her up.

A long, wailing cry filled the darkness, becoming louder.

"What's that sound?" Tianna asked, her eyes wide with fear, and then she breathed in and pointed.

Catty followed her gaze.

A glistening black shadow streaked toward

them with unbelievable speed. A humanlike shape formed in its center, and her father stepped forward, his satin cloak flapping behind him, his hair settling about his shoulders.

"You deceived me, Catty," he said with quiet fury. "We had an agreement to exchange Chris for the Scroll. Now you'll have neither."

CHAPTER THIRTY

"I'll destroy the Scroll before I give it to you," Catty said defiantly, releasing her hold on Vanessa and Serena.

Their hands searched frantically, trying to grab on to her again, but she let them flounder in the mists, knowing with certainty that if she didn't stand against her father now there would be no chance for any of them to return to their homes.

She opened the large, pink shoulder bag and took out the parchment. It twisted angrily, seeming to be alive.

"If you destroy the Scroll," her father said. "You'll destroy the Keeper as well."

She whipped around. "Is that true?"

Chris nodded solemnly. "My life is bound to it."

Her father smiled, seeming to enjoy her dilemma. Then he held out his hand, the white fingers long and smooth, inviting her to surrender the Scroll to him.

Catty glanced at Chris, her heart aching. She had to destroy the Scroll no matter what the cost. She had no choice. The Scroll's curse was too dangerous. It had already killed one man and probably more, and she sensed its power growing.

But there was something more. She feared the manuscript. Its purity, from when it had been created, centuries back, had become polluted. Its power could be used for good or for evil now.

She looked at Chris again, studying his beautiful, sad face, and her resolve weakened.

"Free me," he said, his eyes pleading.

She shook her head. "I don't think I can do that."

"You must do it," Chris whispered.

She bit her lip, wishing the goddess who had helped her once before would suddenly appear and guide her.

"You haven't considered all your options, Catty," her father said in a soothing voice, stepping closer. "If you give me the Scroll, I'll have immeasurable power. That could be to your advantage. I could protect you and your friends. I'll even help you get safely back to your world."

"I don't want your help." Catty tore the moon amulet from her neck and pinched it tightly in her fingers.

"Is your talisman supposed to frighten me?" her father asked with contempt.

"No," she answered boldly. "I need it to destroy the Scroll." She felt compelled to do it at that moment. But did she have the strength?

"Really?" Her father seemed amused. His reaction wasn't the one she had anticipated. She had thought he would try to stop her, but he didn't move.

She glanced up at the strange night sky, so cold and indifferent, as she searched for the moon.

When a Regulator had told her before to destroy the Scroll, he had directed her to reflect the moonlight from her amulet onto the manuscript. But where was the moon? Her stomach tightened, remembering.

"That's right, Catty," her father said, sensing her thoughts. "Nefandus has no moon. There's really no way for you to destroy the Scroll here, and I'll never let you take it back to earth's realm."

Her shoulders slumped. She had failed miserably. Her father started to take the Scroll from her. It slipped through her fingers.

The last time she had felt that hopeless, a moon goddess disguised as an ordinary woman had come to help her. She sighed, disconsolate, feeling utterly abandoned, but then she remembered the waitress from the Summer Moon Tea Room.

She yanked the Scroll back from her father and pulled the fortune from her pocket.

She read it out loud, "The moonlight is reflected from the beauty within you."

Hope surged through her, and she knew

what she had to do. Her powers might not work here, but nothing could stop the strength of the moon; its luminescence glowed inside her and through her.

She glanced up at her father. The force of his anger made her step backward.

Quickly, she placed the Scroll on the ground and knelt next to it, holding it in place with her knees. The parchment vibrated ominously, fighting for survival. The delicate artwork took on a cold and corrupt feeling, as if the knowledge contained within it were sinister and evil.

But then she thought of Chris again and looked at him through tear-blurred eyes.

He smiled thinly, as if he understood her regret and sorrow. "Quickly," he whispered. "It has to be done."

"I can't," she said, shaking her head, knowing she would also end his life.

"Do it, Catty," he answered. "Please don't make me suffer more. I need peace."

Catty nodded, then concentrated, hot tears running down her cheeks. She imagined the lustrous beauty of the moon and pictured its milky gleam.

She felt, more than heard, her father's footsteps and knew he was rushing to stop her, but before he reached her, she waved her hand across the air. A blue moon glow emanated from her palm. She grasped her amulet and reflected the eerie light onto the manuscript. The parchment writhed and buckled, releasing toxic fumes as it began to smolder. Silver flames licked its borders.

Her father shouted with rage, but his angry words were drowned by the unholy shriek from the Scroll.

Catty felt suddenly dizzy and nauseated, not wanting to look, but unable to pull her gaze away. The intricate artwork began to untangle. The decorative tendrils and ivy squirmed into the air with malicious intent, attacking her. If she hadn't felt so violently terrified she would have admired its savage beauty.

Then the parchment split open, releasing unfathomable power and magic.

She stood and staggered back, suddenly

understanding what she had done. Chris had warned her that the heir always made a fatal error, and now she had made hers. She could feel the life draining from her. The Scroll was stronger after all, and it had turned on her.

CHAPTER THIRTY-ONE

WHATEVER ENTITY EXISTED in the brilliant light now focused its pure hate on Catty, ready to devour her. It thundered through her ferociously. Suddenly, she sensed that the darkness from her father and the Scroll were only unexplored strengths that she had to learn to integrate into her own. She no longer feared the dark.

As the Scroll's energy continued to throb inside her, she sensed her father's fear and knew that he understood her new, terrifying role of annihilating evil. She symbolized the absolute force of the divine, her power uncompromising and direct. She was the destroyer.

The light disappeared, leaving her breathless. She gasped, trying to find her natural rhythm of breathing, and looked down. The parchment burned now as if it had been an ordinary manuscript. Thin tendrils of bitter smoke twisted into the air from the ashes.

Chris was fading, his image flickering in the breeze, a suggestion of the person he had been centuries back seeming to eclipse the person he had become.

"I'm sorry," she whispered.

But he didn't seem angry: he stared at her as if seeing her for the first time, his eyes full of gratitude. "You're the embodiment of the Scroll now, Catty," he said reverentially. "My job is complete. No heir before you has had the courage to do what you did. The Prophecy has been fulfilled."

His voice continued even though he was now

only a sinuous shaft of golden light. "Only the true heir will have a heart brave enough to destroy the Scroll before setting out on its path. That's the tenth step. The others before you were too afraid to destroy the manuscript. They relied on its power rather than the power within themselves."

Catty sensed her father slipping closer, and she turned to face him. "I have a power that works in Nefandus now," she warned, her strength rising in challenge.

"Dea, certe," he whispered in awe. "Assuredly a goddess. My daughter, you have fulfilled a prophecy, but a dark one. I will see you again soon. *Citius venit periculum cum contemnatur.*"

He lifted his hand, and then a vortex of radiant blackness burst around him, and he disappeared.

A rush of terror filled Catty, her father's threat growing inside her. "Danger comes quickly when it isn't feared," she said, translating his Latin.

She sensed Chris reaching out to comfort her, but his touch was no more than air breezing across her face. He had vanished, and only a shimmering, golden glow remained.

Without warning, a very real Kyle burst through the golden curtain of light.

Catty blinked and shook her head. It had to be her imagination, she thought, but then she realized that Kyle had just stepped through the portal.

He looked up at her, surprised. "Catty?"

Immediately she understood that he had come back to Nefandus to find her.

"The portal's open!" she shouted with joy as she ran back to her friends. She grabbed on to them, shoving them forward, and pushed them through the gate. She dove after them, taking Kyle with her.

Moments later, she stood on a street in Chinatown, leaning against Kyle. A cold breeze blew blackened scraps of firecracker paper around them.

Vanessa glanced at *The Los Angeles Times,* in a newspaper bin. "We've been gone nine days!" she shrieked, and started running to her car.

"How are we going to explain this to our parents?" Serena asked, sprinting after her, Tianna and Jimena close behind.

"Are you coming?" Vanessa cried over her shoulder to Catty.

"No." Catty looked at Kyle. "I'll see you tomorrow."

Kyle seemed flustered. "It can never work between us, Catty."

"Those weren't exactly the words I had expected to hear you say," she said, slipping her arms around him.

"Nefandus is my home," he explained. "So if I try to kiss someone who isn't from that realm, I'll absorb her power. It's a curse the Atrox put on the *servi,* so that even if we escape we can never find love, because we'll slowly kill anyone we care to."

Catty finally understood his hesitation. She brazenly drew him closer. "I'm not scared," she whispered, her lips brushing against his. "I've finally accepted my dark side, the part of me I inherited from my father, so I guess I'm half like you now, maybe more."

He smiled, then kissed her lightly, testing her theory. When nothing happened, he kissed her again, his lips soft and sweet on hers.

Happiness rushed through her, but it was mixed with a sense of foreboding. Now she knew her destiny was, one day, to face the Atrox alone.

Coming soon: the bad-boy companion series to

DAUGHTERS OF THE MOON

barbarian

"OBIE," A DEEP VOICE called.

Startled, Obie turned.

Two guys in faded black concert T-shirts crouched nearby beneath a dry, dusty oleander bush.

"The *Barbie*-girl is looking for you." The skinny one pointed, and his studded leather cuff slipped down his bone-thin arm.

Obie frowned and turned.

Kirsten Ashton stood near the row of discarded desks. She smiled and fanned her hand in a silly wave. Her shining curls and glossy, pink lips clashed with the stark black eyeliner, straight hair, and major attitudes of the girls hanging out in Smoker's Alley.

She clutched her notebook against her chest and moved softly through the weeds, waving hi to everyone she passed, oblivious to their cold, silent stares. She had the regal confidence of all popular kids and assumed she'd be accepted anywhere.

She stopped in front of Obie. "I called your name three times. Didn't you hear me?" she asked sweetly, and cocked her head.

"No." Obie wondered what she wanted with him. She sat behind him in history class and usually acted as if he weren't even there. Not that he cared.

"I love your new song," she said with a flirty smile. "I heard "Time Trap" on the radio this morning. It's going to be a big hit."

"Thanks," he replied, only half listening to her. The feeling of alarm that had enveloped him earlier was fading, but he was still on edge, distracted by even the slightest movement around him.

"Your music makes me feel so much longing." She brushed a hand through her platinum-blond hair. Her silver nail polish matched the lines painted around her eyes. "Where do you get your inspiration?"

He shrugged, and, before Kirsten could say more, the warning bell rang, signaling the end of the lunch break. Kids stamped out their cigarettes and started back to class. Kirsten joined them.

But Obie didn't want to push into the crush of kids sneaking back onto campus before the final bell. He charged off in the other direction and lunged between two overgrown Arizona cypresses. The scratchy branches snapped and cracked as he emerged from the other side and then sprinted across the basketball courts toward the front of the school.

Obie turned onto a breezeway and dodged around the kids hurrying to class. His boots pounded the concrete with a thumping noise louder than that of the rowdy yells and laughter.

He took the next corner too quickly and slammed into Allison Taylor. She had been standing with her friends, and now they broke apart, startled by his sudden appearance.

"Sorry." He caught Allison around the waist before she fell. Her dark hair swept over his chest, and her flowery perfume spun around him. He breathed in her fragrance like a thief, and let his hands linger on her soft, warm skin. She reminded him of someone he had known before. "I didn't mean to knock you over," he said, apologizing.

Allison stepped back and looked down. "It's only a foot. I'll get a new one."

Her friends laughed.

She wore leather sandals, silver toe rings, and beaded strings of hemp around her thin ankles. A bruise was causing a swelling on the top of her foot. He felt like whisking her into his arms and carrying her to one of the picnic benches in the quad to make sure she was okay, but he controlled the impulse; such things weren't done here.

Allison turned back to her friends as if Obie weren't even standing there.

"I just got a chill," Allison said and rubbed the gooseflesh on her tanned arms. "Someone must have walked over my grave."

"That didn't give you the chill," Obie said, intruding again.

Allison's friends stared at him. Arielle adjusted her halter, as if Obie's presence made her uncomfortable, and Caitlin tugged nervously at her earring, waiting to see what Allison would do.

"Are you telling me it was the thrill of seeing you?" Allison asked, breaking the tension.

Arielle laughed too loudly, and Caitlin continued to stare.

"As if." Allison rolled her eyes and turned away from him again.

Obie continued slowly down the outside corridor to the other side of the classroom door, kids shoving around him, and settled back against the wall, alone. He turned back to watch Allison. She was the most popular girl at Turney High, and kids gathered around her as if she were a movie star handing out autographs. What would she have done if he had told her the true reason for her gooseflesh? He smirked, imagining her reaction, but in the end she wouldn't have believed him, and it would only have given her one more reason to make fun of him.

"She'll never go out with you," a sulky voice whispered. Kirsten stood beside him, spreading brown gloss on her lips. He hadn't heard her sidle up next to him.

"Like I care," he answered.

"Don't lie to me." Kirsten seemed annoyed. "Your crush is so obvious."

"Crush?"

"Anyone can see you're crazy in like with her."

"You're wrong," he said, finally understanding her choice of words. "I don't like her." No girl was worth the risk. He couldn't change what fate had made him.